The Troubled Thoughts Of A Teenager

On Newsstands Now:

TRUE STORY
and
TRUE CONFESSIONS
Magazines

True Story and *True Confessions* are the world's largest and best-selling women's romance magazines. They offer true-to-life stories to which women can relate.

Since 1919, the iconic *True Story* has been an extraordinary publication. The magazine gets its inspiration from the hearts and minds of women, and touches on those things in life that a woman holds close to her heart, like love, loss, family and friendship.

True Confessions, a cherished classic first published in 1922, looks into women's souls and reveals their deepest secrets.

To subscribe, please visit our website:
www.TrueRenditionsLLC.com or call **(212) 922-9244**

To find the TRUES at your local store, please visit:
www.WheresMyMagazine.com

The Troubled Thoughts Of A Teenager

From the Editors
Of *True Story* And
True Confessions

Published by True Renditions, LLC

True Renditions, LLC
105 E. 34th Street, Suite 141
New York, NY 10016

ISBN: 978-1-938877-92-6

Visit us on the web at www.truerenditionsllc.com.

Contents

CHEERLEADER TRAGEDY
The All-American sport can be dangerous

I had wanted to be a cheerleader from as far back as I could remember. My big sister, Hillary, had been one, and I was always in awe watching her practice or perform at basketball games. Hillary was my hero, and I always looked up to her. I was so lucky to have a big sister like her while I was growing up.

At the games, I always paid far more attention to the cheerleaders than I did to the athletes who were working their butts off trying to win the game. And the following day, my voice was always hoarse and my throat scratchy, because I'd screamed my head off along with the cheerleading squad. I knew every routine, every cheer word for word, and I wasn't afraid to show it.

I loved everything about the cheerleaders. I liked their uniforms in bright school colors with little flippy skirts that twirled and danced along with the girls. My mom even sewed one for me when I was little, so I could practice at home along with Hillary. I must have outgrown several of those before I got to be a real cheerleader with a real uniform.

I loved the pom-poms that Hillary sometimes let me use as she taught me a particular move or just let me dance while I waved them all around, practicing kicks and jumps I'd seen the cheerleaders do. I especially loved the squad's energy and their stunts, the back flips, the flyers who were thrown high into the air and then neatly caught by the others on the floor, the pyramids, the splits and the kicks—everything they did.

"That's going to be me, someday," I would say again and again to my parents, my sister, and anyone else who would listen.

So when I was still just a kid, Hillary suggested to my parents that they let me take gymnastics. It was an ideal preparation for cheering. Not only did it keep me in great physical shape, but I truly loved it. It was all a part of working up to my dream: as soon as I became a high school freshman, I would try out for the cheerleading squad.

Competition to get on the squad was always tough, and a freshman almost never made it on her first try. But I was so determined that I worked my butt off practicing not just at the after-school prep sessions, but for hours at home, too.

Hillary had graduated college, married, and lived with her husband and my two nieces halfway across the country. But I talked to her often, and definitely during our practice sessions for tryouts.

Practice sessions were grueling, and, by the time we were finished, each afternoon, we sprawled out on the mats sweating like crazy and breathing hard, reaching for our bottles of energy drinks or water and guzzling it down. There were only four slots available on the team, and twelve of us were trying out so competition was fierce. And even though we all tried to be friendly and encourage each other, each girl was one another's rival.

Three of us were freshmen, my best bud, Felicity, and this new girl named Dawn. I introduced Felicity and myself to her at the first practice. She had a heavy southern drawl and told us about having to move to our town from some tiny place we'd never heard of.

"We move all the time," Dawn told us. "It's because of my dad's job. I'm pretty much used to being the new kid on the block, the one everyone points at and whispers about behind their backs. I suppose it's my fault," she added. "I don't make friends easily, and I've always been kind of a loner."

"Well, that doesn't fit the description of someone trying out for the cheerleading squad her first week in a new school," I told her. "That's definitely not something a loner would do. Give yourself some credit for even trying out. The competition is tough, and very few freshmen get in the first time."

"Yup," Felicity put in. "And it looks like we three are the only freshmen trying out this year. We could all bomb and have to go through this all again next year."

"That means the other nine candidates have been around awhile, and we haven't, which could work against us. Why are you trying out before you even know anybody?" I asked. "That seems like a pretty brave thing to do."

"Or a pretty stupid thing to do," Dawn countered. "I'll probably fall flat on my face and totally humiliate myself. But I promised Mom I would give it my best shot."

"Was your mom a cheerleader?" I asked.

"Was she ever!" Dawn replied. "She was team captain for three years, and her squad won a ton of trophies, which she never lets me forget. And she's always been super pushy trying to get me more involved in school activities, whereas I'd rather just go to my classes, do homework, and study and get good grades. I do get good grades but that's never been enough to satisfy, Mom. She's been telling me all my life that I have to become a cheerleader, and if I don't it'll be letting her down big time. That's why it's so important I get in."

Felicity and I exchanged a look. "You should be able to do what you want, not follow some life plan your mom made for you that you don't even agree with," Felicity said.

I agreed with Felicity, but I didn't think the relationship Dawn had with her mom was any of our business. And I thought about the

2

performances I'd seen from Dawn so far. It was obvious her heart wasn't in it. Her moves were lackluster, definitely in need of more polish and a big boost in energy. And she needed to smile more. Part of the time she was biting her lower lip, looking worried and miserable at the same time. She was klutzy, stumbled a lot, and suffered a fall that looked like it would bring on major pain.

Felicity had noticed all these things about Dawn as well.

"I don't even know why she's bothering to try out," she whispered to me in the locker room. "She obviously has no talent and no clue about what's involved in being a cheerleader."

"I feel kind of sorry for her," I said. "She's obviously trying out just to please her bossy mom. And from what I've seen, I don't think she has the slightest chance of making the squad. I imagine she'll feel humiliated when she doesn't get picked."

Dawn's performance at the next day's practice was similarly bad. She fell twice, ended up stepping on someone's hand and, more than once, and moved left when she should have gone right. She was even behind on the words of the cheers, like she didn't know them without a prompt from the others. There was no way she was magically going to improve in time for the actual tryouts in just two more days.

It was obvious to everyone that Dawn didn't have what it takes. The team captain, a tall redhead named Lanie, was obviously furious and asked all of us newbies to stick around awhile after practice. So all twelve of us sat side by side on a bench while Lanie walked back and forth in front of us. The other cheerleaders were just a few feet away whispering among themselves.

At last Lanie spoke.

"Nobody ever said cheerleading was easy. And if any of you new tryouts think it is, then the best thing you can do for yourself and for us is to walk out that door and never look back. You're wasting our time, and you're wasting your own."

The rest of the squad stopped whispering and came over to stand behind their captain. Their expressions, such a contrast from their smiles during practice, were now stone cold and serious. Several of them had their arms crossed in front of them, a few scowled, definitely not encouraging body language.

"Cheerleading is hard work," Lanie continued. "It's more than just a sport, it's an art form. It requires physical strength, coordination, the ability to remember every move to every routine as well as all the words to every cheer, and you're meant to get it right every single time." She took a deep breath. "When we're out there trying to lead our team to victory we have to give one hundred percent. On the night of a big game is not the time for insecurity, for hesitation, for klutziness."

I watched as Lanie's gaze settled on Dawn. "Maybe some of you just aren't cut out to be cheerleaders," she said, her eyes still on the new girl. I felt embarrassed and uncomfortable that Lanie had singled her out like that. It didn't seem necessary, and it wasn't very nice. I had heard Lanie was a tough team leader. I hadn't expected her to be any other way. But now, all the other cheerleaders behind her were staring at Dawn as well. I chanced a glance at her and saw that her face was flushed bright red. Some of it might be from the workout, but the rest was probably from being singled out and humiliated in front of the others.

"Now, tomorrow is our last practice before the tryouts on Friday," Lanie continued. "As you know, there are only four spots on the squad, and there are twelve of you." She looked up and down our row. "But I expect you all, all," she repeated, "to give us outstanding performances on Friday. I want you to make it tough for us"—she gestured behind her at the other girls—"tough for us to decide whom those four will be. Now, go home and practice. And when you think you're done, practice some more. See you all tomorrow."

We all stood up and began gathering our things. I had thought Lanie was finished but I was wrong.

"Hey, Southern girl," I heard her call. "Dawn, isn't it? I want to talk to you. Privately," she added, pointedly looking at the rest of us so we'd clear out.

"I wonder what she's going to say to Dawn?" I asked Felicity as we left the gym. "That was a pretty harsh speech back there and did you see the way she and the others kept looking at Dawn? She like totally humiliated her."

"But you know what Lanie said is true. If one of us just doesn't cut it, then she should leave. And it's obvious to all of us that Dawn is not cheerleader material. I doubt if she ever will be," Felicity added.

Still, I felt bad for Dawn, and when I noticed her sitting on the stairs in front of the school, I went over and sat beside her. Her face was still red and her eyes were puffy. It was obvious she'd been crying.

"Hey," I said. "For what it's worth, I still think you're really brave trying out the way you are. I mean not only being a freshman, but also being new to our school, and our whole town. I can't even imagine how I would feel being yanked out of school and home and friends every few years the way you are."

"But she's right, you know? What Lanie said? I really don't have the talent to be one of you."

"What did she say to you after the rest of us left?" I asked.

"Oh, she really lit into me," Dawn said. "I mean she was actually mean about it. Said I shouldn't even bother showing up for tryouts tomorrow because they had already decided I wouldn't get it. 'They' meaning her and her teammates, I guess."

"So does that mean you're not coming to tryouts?" I asked.

To be honest, in light of what she'd just told me, there really was no point in her being there. And even though I thought earlier that Lanie was too hard on Dawn, I felt it might have been a kindness taking her aside and be brutally honest about her not having a chance to get on the squad. It would save her the humiliation of performing solo in front of everybody and making a total mess of the cheer and herself.

"I don't know what I'm going to tell my mom," Dawn said, her voice trembling a bit. "I'm not going to tell her tonight that I didn't make the squad."

"Putting that off won't make it any easier the next day," I said. "And wouldn't she expect you to be practicing tonight?"

Dawn gave a low, almost eerie moan. "I dread going home," she said. "I might as well just kill myself."

Okay, that scared me. I'd never heard anyone threaten suicide before when they sounded serious the way Dawn did.

"Do you want me to go home with you?" I asked. "To be there when you tell your mom?" I had expected to spend the evening practicing, but I felt like if there was anything I could do or say to help her out; I should at try.

But she just shook her head and stood up.

"No, that's okay," she said. "But thanks for the offer." She walked down a few steps before turning around to look at me again. "You know, you're the only student who's been truly nice to me here." And then, before I could respond, she left.

So I pushed thoughts of Dawn aside—I truly didn't expect to see her at tryouts the next day—ended up practicing all evening like I'd planned, and then called my sister, Hillary, for some last minute moral support.

"I know you're going to make it," she said. "You've been preparing for this most of your life!"

I thanked her for her confidence in me, and then, I went to bed.

But I was still really nervous. Between that and thinking about my conversation with Dawn, I hardly slept a wink all night.

People don't kill themselves for not making cheerleader, do they?

But I worried when Dawn wasn't in school the next day. Finally, I confided in Felicity about our after-school conversation.

"Oh, people say stuff like that all the time," Felicity reassured me. "I'm sure it was just a figure of speech, and she didn't really mean it. And I remember reading once that the people who really commit suicide are usually the quiet ones who don't talk about it ahead of time."

So I felt better and was even able to push my worries about Dawn aside like I had during my practice the night before.

Tryouts were after school in the gymnasium, and it felt like I'd never had such a long day in my entire life. My best friend, Felicity, noticed it, too.

"Hey, chill," she said to me at lunch. "I know you want this more than anything in your life. From what I've noticed about the other girls, you're by far the best."

It was so sweet of her to say that, especially since she was trying out, too. And she was good, really good. I suddenly found myself thinking: What if she gets on the squad and I don't?

But once I got to the gym, I felt my confidence return. I watched the other girls who went up and performed before me and some of them were awesome. But when it was my turn, I said to myself, "I'm awesome, too." And I got myself really believing it. Also, I was determined that, win or lose, I was going to have fun. And if I didn't make it this year, there were still another three years of high school.

I stood in front of the other girls, the ones who were already on the squad, the team captain, the coach, and the ones vying for one of those available spots, just like me.

Here I go Hillary, I whispered to myself and, suddenly, I felt like I was with Hillary in our backyard, and there was nothing I couldn't do.

I raised my arms and shouted, "Ready? Okay!" Then I launched into the dance and for the next three and half minutes, I was totally in control. I did my flips, my kicks, my splits, grinning like crazy 'cause I was having a ball. After I'd done my grand finish, everyone cheered wildly. At least, I believed they did. But I was flying high because I knew I hadn't made a single mistake in the routine.

I walked back to the benches and sat next to Felicity. She had gone before me and did a terrific job herself.

"You were great," she said and gave me a hug.

I was sweating and breathing hard, but I felt truly exhilarated. I refused to let myself think that I would be one of the losers. I was gonna win, win, win! I just felt it.

I totally nailed the routine, I kept telling myself, still high on my rush of adrenalin. I'll earn a place on the squad.

Just then Felicity leaned over and whispered to me, "Look who's here."

I followed her glance behind us and up high on the bleachers to the last row. There, looking small and unimportant, which must have been exactly how she felt, was Dawn.

"Has she been here the whole time?" I asked.

"I think so. I saw a few of Lanie's glares directed up there."

"She's just torturing herself by being here," I whispered back.

Dawn wasn't looking at us, so I couldn't wave as an acknowledgement

6

of her presence. I turned back to the last few tryouts and paid rapt attention to my competition.

And then, just like that, we'd all done our routines—all eleven of us. Tryouts were over, and we'd all survived, well, maybe not Dawn, but now, we just had to wait for all the points to be tallied and listen to the four names that would soon be called.

The cheerleaders, the captain, and the coach had taken notes as each of us performed. Now, they all had their heads together to decide. They must have deliberated for twenty minutes, at least.

Then Lanie stood up, a sheet of paper in her hands, and walked over to stand in front of us. She spared a quick glance to the bleachers high above us, then focused her attention on the eleven girls whose, if they were anything like me, hearts were beating fast and had stomachs that felt full of butterflies. Lanie cleared her throat.

"Ladies, first of all I want to thank all of you for trying out," she said. "We saw some awesome performances out there, today. So awesome, in fact, that we had an extremely difficult time picking only four of you. I think you should give yourselves a big hand for the work and the sheer determination that has been so evident right from the start."

She started clapping, and we all joined in, whooping it up for ourselves as well, the lot of us loud and enthusiastic, and definitely sounding like the cheerleaders we hoped to be.

"I'm going to call out four names," Lanie said once we were quiet again. "And I want each of you to come up here and stand next to me. First of all, sophomore Kayla Greenstone."

Kayla screamed and bounced over to her place next to Lanie while the rest of us applauded.

"Next, we have junior Terri Nazer." Another scream and more applause. I knew that both of these girls were awesome.

"Next we have senior Nikki Christensen."

Felicity and I exchanged looks and held tight to each other's hands. We knew there was no longer any chance we'd both be on the squad. But would either of us make it? Or would we both be passed over and have to wait until next year to try again?

"And finally," Lanie said with much drama, "although in our school's history a freshman only rarely makes it onto our squad, this year, we find ourselves with an exceptionally good candidate for our final slot." She paused, and Felicity and I squeezed our hands together even harder. Lanie was torturing us before she'd announce the final name.

Then there it was, the final name sounding as though I was hearing it through a conch shell I'd picked up on the beach. The name was mine!!

7

Immediately, Felicity and I threw our arms around each other, and then I jumped up and ran over to take the last position on the squad. I had done it. I had really done it!

"Yeah team!" I shouted, pumping my fist into the air. "Yeah team," the other three newbies responded. Pretty soon, everyone on the original squad was yelling it and jumping up and down right along with us. It was truly the most exciting moment in my life.

Then Lanie was talking again, and we had to quiet down so she could be heard.

"I want to thank all the rest of you girls again for trying out. Just because you didn't make it this year, doesn't mean we won't want to see you trying out again next year. Go, team, go!" she yelled, before joining the rest of us.

I wanted to tell Felicity how sorry I was that she wouldn't be joining me as a cheerleader, but before any one of the girls who hadn't made it could even stand up, I caught sight of a movement on the bleachers above. Dawn was slowly making her way down to the gym floor, one step at a time, her gaze fixed on Lanie, who was standing pretty much in the middle of our group, still congratulating the four who had made it. She was wearing some kind of cheerleading uniform, not our school's. It didn't even fit her well. I wondered if it was one of her mom's old uniforms. But it was a totally bad idea playing that kind of dress up.

I could tell when Lanie looked up and saw Dawn walking toward us. We parted to clear her a path to our team captain. That was before any of us saw the gun in Dawn's hand.

"What are you doing here?" Lanie asked her tone harsh enough to cut through stone. "I thought I told you to just save yourself the humiliation."

Then Lanie's eyes widened as she saw the weapon Dawn's right hand held dangling at her side.

"You made fun of me in front of everyone," Dawn accused. "Do you even know how important it was for me to make it onto your squad? My mom's going to kill me when I tell her what happened. Or better yet, she might come back and kill you!"

Dawn raised her arm and pointed the gun at Lanie.

Everybody was pretty much glued to her place in shock.

"Dawn, you don't want to hurt anyone, really you don't," Lanie told her.

One of the girls started rooting around for something inside her bag.

"Get your hands where I can see them," Dawn said, suddenly turning the gun on her. When the girl ignored what she said and pulled out a cell phone, Dawn shot her. Just like that.

8

The girl fell back, a red stain spreading across the front of her uniform. I couldn't tell for sure, but she didn't move, and to me she looked dead.

"Dawn, what are you doing?" I screamed, getting her attention. "We talked about this yesterday. I thought you were going to be all right. Didn't you talk to your mom last night?"

Slowly, she walked over to where I stood. I could see some of the other girls fanning out, trying to get behind her. Many were crying.

Dawn's eyes were like ice as she came up to me and held the gun to one side of my head. I could feel the pressure of the cold metal barrel, and I stood as if petrified by my fear.

"Noooo!" I heard someone scream. Felicity?

I kept my gaze on Dawn's face and watched in stunned surprise as her eyes softened, and she lowered the gun.

"You were nice to me," she said in a voice with no detectable emotion. "You were the only one. You can stay," she said. "You can stay on the team."

I wasn't at all sure what she meant. But when she turned away from me, she seemed to remember she hadn't finished with Lanie. She held the gun up to the side of her head, the same as she'd done to me.

"Proud of your girls, are you?" she asked. "All so much better than me, aren't they?" Her gaze swept over the others. She looked at the other three newly chosen members, huddled together, two of them crying, the other one on her knees praying.

Pop, pop, pop! It sounded like firecrackers. But the three new girls had gone down, one with each bullet. I found myself with the terrifyingly insane thought that Dawn was a good shot.

"They were better than me, weren't they?" she asked Lanie. "You chose them, but now they're gone. Just like that, three new vacancies on the squad." Dawn remembered the other girl, the one who had gotten out her cell phone. "Oops, forgot her," Dawn put a hand up to her mouth and giggled. "Maybe four vacancies."

She turned around and faced the other tryouts behind her, the ones who hadn't made it.

"How many more slots should I create for you, my fellow tryouts? I could get each one of you on that squad if I wanted to. It's all in the numbers and, believe me, I have lots of bullets."

All those girls started crying, too. "But you don't want a bunch of crybabies, do you Lanie?" she asked, turning back to her. "You're way too tough to put up with that."

I had been slowly and carefully moving around the gym, trying to put myself behind Dawn, but it was tough with the way she kept turning back and forth between the two groups.

With her attention on Lanie again, I moved the last few yards until

I was behind her. I had the idea, crazy as it might be, that if I could get behind Dawn and grab her, that I could take her down. I was stronger than she was. I knew that from all our practice sessions and my years of gymnastics training.

Lanie saw me—heck, they all did—and I hoped they were planning to help distract Dawn long enough for me to pull her down.

"Listen, Dawn," Lanie started. "I'm sorry I was so hard on you. I know now that I shouldn't have treated you that way. I was very wrong to do so."

Her gaze seemed locked onto the sight of the gun pointed in her face. I thought it was pretty brave of her to say anything at all. I knew Dawn especially wanted to punish the leader. I only hoped that I could do something before Lanie ended up dead.

"It's not too late, you know, Dawn," Lanie continued. "I could spend time with you, train you until you're ready. I'm going to have to pick new girls for the squad. I could pick you for my first choice, what do you say girls?"

She glanced over her shoulder at the others who were still standing.

As for me, I refused to look at the girls who had been gunned down. I was pretty sure none of them were breathing, and I didn't want to lose my nerve by checking them out again. I threw a pleading look at the girls on the bench behind our shooter. I prayed they would all help me when the time came.

Dawn laughed at Lanie.

"You think I can't tell you're a lying witch?" she asked her. "From the very first day you had me pegged for a loser. You had no intention of letting me on the squad. Not then and not now. You just came up with all those lies so I won't shoot you. Okay, so you say I'm your first new choice, huh? Well, guess what? I'm gonna shoot you, anyway."

That was when I launched myself at Dawn and grabbed both arms, pinning them to her sides, but not before she managed to fire off another shot. I heard at least three people scream. Lanie, Dawn, and Felicity. Felicity, blessedly, ran over and yanked the gun out of Dawn's hand.

"Anyone with a cell phone," I yelled. "Call 911. Do it, now!"

By that time there were several of us holding Dawn down. She was kicking and screaming and trying to claw and bite her way to freedom. But we all kept her down, anyway, although it seemed like forever until we heard the sirens getting close.

There was a crowd around Lanie, but I couldn't see how badly she was hurt. All I knew was that she was still alive. A few of the girls went outside to tell the cops and the medical people where to find us. The police had Dawn expertly under control and handcuffed in a matter of minutes.

They pulled her up to her feet, and it was while they were dragging her toward, the door that she began yelling at me.

"You shouldn't have stopped me," she said. "I was going to shoot myself for the finale. It was to be my last tryout ever. You should have let me do it; you should have let me. . . ."

And then, she was gone, on her way to the police station no doubt. I actually felt sorry for her in a way. Now that I knew it was probably her mother whose expectations had pushed her to the point of madness.

As I had feared, the four girls were dead. But the paramedics told us Lanie was going to recover from the gunshot wound. Unfortunately, the shot had gone wild when I grabbed Dawn. It had had shattered Lanie's right kneecap, effectively putting an end to her cheerleading career. But later, when a few of us visited Lanie in the hospital, she couldn't stop thanking me for saving her life and maybe a lot of other lives, too.

It's been rough on all of us. Thankfully, our town managed to keep this out of the media. Only our town's weekly reported it. The editor's editorial said that he didn't want us to be exploited, so there wouldn't be any follow-up articles. I was glad. Although I didn't have to see pictures in the newspaper, I kept seeing them in my mind.

Our school closed for the remainder of the week, so we could all just chill at home. Most of us would have been too numb to do much, anyway. The four girls were given one huge funeral together. I'll never forget the sight of those four coffins lined up side by side in the front of the church.

Unfortunately, we still didn't have money in the budget for costly new security measures, so nothing changed. I tried not to think that the whole thing could happen all over again. After awhile, the word went around that Dawn was in a psychiatric hospital, getting the help she so badly needed.

It was awhile before anyone mentioned what we knew we'd have to go through all over again. Cheerleader tryouts. We picked a new team captain, but named Lanie an honorary member for the remainder of her senior year. She and I actually got to be good friends. And Felicity was one of the other newbies who made the team, so we were together after all.

I know Mom and Hillary worried that I wouldn't want to cheer after what had happened. But I still do, and I'm doing a fine job. Who knows, team captain, someday? Nothing surprises me, anymore.

THE END

RUNAWAY TEEN

When we were seniors in high school, my friend Rebecca—aided and abetted by Mandy, her best friend and worst influence—ran away to live with a guy she herself might have called a creep, if she hadn't been smitten with him. He was much older than Rebecca, a recovering drug addict, and ironically, he had trained her to be a peer counselor at the drop-in center where she volunteered. They'd been seeing each other in secret for some months; I had never met him and, until a few weeks before she left, didn't even know he existed.

Rebecca and I weren't super close, but her sudden departure amazed me. How could a seventeen-year-old A-student jeopardize a potentially interesting adult life, far from our dreary Long Island suburb, for some aging local hippie so upset about the whole situation he was thinking of going back to drugs?

Rebecca left her friends feeling confused, guilty, and partly responsible. Perhaps we should have seen it coming; words and phrases like "I can't take it at home anymore!" provided vague clues. But in our youthful subculture, the code of conduct forbade asking parents and teachers for help. If we had suspicions, we never discussed them with one another, much less with any adults.

The situation was unthinkable to begin with. Rebecca was a "good girl." She wore her black hair long and chastely parted down the middle. She carried her books tightly and protectively against her breasts. She wore a uniform of blouses and skirts in dark solids, with feminine pumps or neat loafers. Though she sometimes fell prey to the jeans and T-shirt style of the day, the natural look was not entirely natural on her—she was too pressed and clean.

Rebecca was thin-skinned in every sense of the word—a delicate filigree of tiny blue veins ran through her translucent skin. On the rare occasions she wore a low-cut blouse, she seemed as vulnerable as a newborn white mouse. She was like Snow White, falling prey to the shrunken, gloomy, and uni-browed Mandy; Mandy of the gypsy earrings and annoying stammer, who held out pretty poison apples of depression to her friend and follower.

I knew something was wrong at Rebecca's home, but I didn't know what. Our conversations over bland cafeteria lunches were not revealing. We didn't trash our families or gossip about other kids. Mostly, she and I shared sticks of chewing gum, along with twin passions for French class and folk music. Once in a great while she'd shock me with something uncharacteristic, like the time she confessed to smoking weed with Mandy behind the lake at Grant Park.

"Mandy got the stuff," she said mysteriously. "It was kind of creepy back there. Empty beer cans and dog poo."

"Ew," I remarked, nose wrinkling. "So, what was it like?"

"Nothing special. Basically it was all about the idea of doing something illegal."

Rebecca never discussed boys with me, except perhaps to remark upon how cute some rock star was. I supposed she had even less sexual experience than I, which was next to none. To speak of yearnings would have been too intimate for our cordial friendship. Once, when I mentioned my frustration with Jake—a boy who seemed to think we were going together, when in fact we had never actually gone anywhere or done anything with or to each other—her silence betrayed her discomfort, and I swiftly changed the subject.

Rebecca studied and obeyed her mother and father, while I was prone to small acts of rebellion, sporadic blips on the parental danger meter. A closet hellion, I danced around the label of "problem child." Yet I was never kept after class, never took a single puff off a friend's marijuana pipe, and never brought home an unacceptable report card. And to my chagrin, I wasn't dating. Though I frequently stayed out as late as five a.m. with my friends, as long as I let my parents know where I was, they didn't mind.

However, I did like to drink illegally purchased cheap white wine, trespass on the beach at night, and participate in Chinese fire drills—stopping the car at a red light, getting out, running around the car screaming, and getting back in. I smoked cigarettes on the school lawn, frequently told my parents to go to hell (and occasionally worse), applied too much makeup in the girl's room at school, and sometimes skipped gym. Fairly normal teenage stuff, I rationalized. Of course, next to Rebecca, I looked like a juvenile delinquent—until she began sneaking out to see her boyfriend from the drop-in center.

At some point I heard about this guy from other friends. At once, I was shocked and scared to death by the news: he was so old, their meetings so clandestine, and they had to be "doing it." I couldn't imagine those delicate little hands with their baby-pink nails and network of tiny capillaries holding onto some sweaty, throbbing, hairy, huge, adult maleness. The very idea gave me the dry heaves.

One day, Rebecca phoned and breathlessly asked if she could tell her mother she was staying at my house for the weekend.

"I don't know," I demurred. "I don't think I can do that. I'm not a very good liar."

"Oh, come on. It's not like my mother's going to call your house and check."

"Well, what if she does? What if my mother answers? What if I can't think of anything to say? We'll both get in trouble."

"No we won't!" Her voice was pleading, desperate.

"Rebecca. . .I don't think this is such a good idea."

"Okay, forget it."

"The whole thing, I mean. It's just not a good idea. I'm sorry, okay? But I mean—"

"Just forget it!" Slam. Click. Dial tone.

I could have simply said no, but in that moment, I transformed from a sassy kid into a self-righteous representative of the Moral Majority, Minors Division. While we hadn't shared many secrets before, my refusal to cover for Rebecca caused a rift in our friendship that never healed.

I soon found out that Rebecca had called just about all of her girlfriends for this favor. Only Mandy did as she was asked—weekend after weekend.

Not long afterwards, while standing with Rebecca at her locker at school, I caught a glimpse of some odd belongings she had stashed there.

"What's that?" I asked, noting a bright Guatemalan shawl trimmed with a fringe of brilliant red and orange pompons. There was also a tambourine and some large, rolled-up sheets of paper that might have been posters.

"Oh, it's just some stuff I'm bringing to a friend's house," she mumbled, quickly slamming shut my view of those teenage objects of decor and comfort, the very things an underage runaway would need to rescue from the rubble of childhood. In my gut, I knew which "friend's" house she was talking about. Yet I still couldn't quite picture Rebecca giving herself over to anyone old enough to have a full beard and a shady past.

My guilt over not reporting my suspicions about Rebecca's departure was soon supplanted by hurt at her abandonment of me and the rest of her friends—other than Mandy. I wondered, too, how she could leave behind her little sister—a tiny, whinier version of herself—to fend off two apparently monstrous parents all alone.

Also, it must be said, I was jealous. Rebecca loved a creep, but at least someone loved her back. I ached to be touched; my entire being longed to be loved so much, I thought I might die of loneliness. Because I had experienced sexual abuse at the hands of a stranger more than once, I was both intensely attracted to and deathly afraid of men. No one remotely like my friend's mangy beloved could have succeeded in pulling me away from the dharma and drama of growing up in the proscribed suburban American fashion—finishing school on schedule.

I was also jealous because Rebecca had managed to pull off the ultimate "drop dead" to her mother and father, while I was mired in a familial hate-fest from which there seemed no escape. Though I also dreamed of leaving, the plan was so many years away. I was waiting for that magical day when I would have enough money and enough education and enough this and enough that. What kind of pull did this boyfriend have, to override prospects of future want? What was this lure of sex? Had passion—instead of reason—beckoned to me in those days, could I have bared a vulnerable breast to it?

My immediate reaction to Rebecca's radical departure was to take on the path of goody-goodiness she had abandoned. See, Mom and Dad, you think I'm such a terrible child, but you won't catch me being so irresponsible as to drop out, I'm going to build myself the right kind of life. I'm not going to lose my head over some twenty-eight-year-old loser.

Never mind that it was Rebecca who had won an elusive poetry prize that, as editor of our school's literary magazine, I coveted. . .that she, with her French father coaching her, excelled in the mellifluous language that I adored but stumbled over. . .that she was beautiful in a lustrous-black-mane-and-porcelain-skin way, in contrast to my swarthy complexion and stringy hair. . .that, had she not run away, she could have written her ticket to Harvard or Yale or at least a Seventh Sister, while I'd have to beg a state school to sponsor me, sitting on my mountain of unrealized potential.

Despite all this, I was now feeling mighty superior to my old friend. As her leaving prodded me to strive for better behavior and greater achievement, I strove to remain in denial of a misery that has prompted young people throughout time to take their own departures.

Though I fooled no one—least of all myself—I invested heavily in the appearance of normality. That meant buttoning up and holding on with all my might to maintain some equilibrium in my shaky young life. Devising industrious moneymaking schemes, from tutoring younger kids to painting T-shirts, so that I could go away to university rather than commute to a local school and have to live with a life-sized Punch and Judy show at home. I took on a safe major in English education instead of a coveted M.F.A. in creative writing—a program where I'd have to compete with those more secure in themselves, their abilities, their futures, and their parents' finances.

It meant coming back to live at home after graduation for far too long, while performing years of safe little jobs in safe little business suits. It meant a succession of safe little boyfriends and, eventually, a safe little apartment in a safe little neighborhood. It also meant self-protection and the approval of others that lasted until I was forty years old and my parents were both dead. I never married, never had a family, and never remotely set the world on fire.

15

So, perhaps Rebecca's druggy drug counselor was the best thing that could have happened to her. When the rest of our friends were in college, we'd heard she had gotten her G.E.D and eventually, she and her lover married and had a family. In adulthood, she went back to school. In the end, no harm was done. And today, I have to wonder which one of us, me or Rebecca, was the true runaway.

THE END

I'm only twelve years old
AM I TOO YOUNG
TO BE A MOMMY?

A voice I didn't recognize was shouting, and it seemed as though it was directed toward me.

"Jessica! Hey, Jessica, wait up!"

Trying to make my way through the crowded restaurant to the rest room in the back, I'd silently wished the young girl luck in finding her friend, Jessica. I'd never seen the restaurant in the mall so crowded.

Just as I'd pushed my way between two men dressed in business suits, I'd felt a hard, urgent hand on my shoulder.

"Jessica, didn't you hear me calling you?"

That was when I'd realized that someone had mistaken me for someone named Jessica.

I'd turned around, expecting the girl to express immediately her embarrassment. Instead, she'd stared at me in shock, as if she were seeing a ghost.

"Oh, my God! You're not Jessica!" she exclaimed. The two suits moved a few inches closer, allowing us standing room only.

Just as I'd pushed my way between two men dressed in business suits, I'd felt a hard, urgent hand on my shoulder.

"Jessica, didn't you hear me calling you?"

That was when I'd realized that someone had mistaken me for someone named Jessica.

I'd turned around, expecting the girl to express immediately her embarrassment. Instead, she'd stared at me in shock, as if she were seeing a ghost.

"Oh, my God! You're not Jessica!" she exclaimed. The two suits moved a few inches closer, allowing us standing room only.

I'd smiled at her expression. "No, I'm not Jessica."

"But—" The young girl shook her head, as if dazed. "You've got to meet Jessica. She could be your twin! You two have the same color hair, and your eyes—you've got to meet her!" The girl's voice had faded to an awed whisper. "I think you guys must be sisters. She was adopted, so it's possible."

"No!" My throat had constricted to the point of choking me. I'd swallowed hard, wondering if the girl had noticed the sudden terror in my eyes. "I'm sorry, but you must be mistaken. I wasn't adopted, so it isn't possible."

The girl looked disappointed. "Oh, well. It's creepy, that's all. I'm sorry that I bothered you."

And then, in the blink of an eye, she'd disappeared into the crowd, leaving me shaking and sick with anxiety.

I'd heard people say that everyone had a twin somewhere in the world, so I supposed I could have used that excuse and gone on as if nothing had happened.

But I'd soon found that I couldn't. Curiosity had arisen from the depths of my terror, and, for the first time in a long time, I'd allowed myself to think about something that my parents had brainwashed me into forgetting. I was a grown woman, after all. I was thirty years old, not an impressionable, frightened child of twelve.

I was the only child of ambitious parents, and my life had been laid out for me well before I was born. Both my parents were law students, just finishing law school when I'd come crying into the world. And, as with everything else in their lives, they'd had me at precisely the time that they'd intended.

From then on, it was as though they were following a map. Piano lessons had begun at the age of five were followed by ballet lessons and private tutors. At the age of seven, I'd had to study, while other girls my age were playing with dolls. I hadn't thought that it was odd, though. In fact, I'd tried very hard to be the child that my parents had wanted me to be, because I'd loved them so much. As a result of my academic achievements, I was able to move from the fourth grade to the six grade, skipping the fifth grade entirely.

In the eighth grade, surrounded by kids a year older than me, I'd begun to realize how different I was, and how different my parents were, compared to other parents. It had all started the day I'd met, and become best friends with, Lauren Harris.

Lauren was the total opposite of me, and so were her parents. Her father worked at a factory and, according to Lauren, could be found in a drunken stupor every Friday night through Sunday. Lauren's mother was a tired waitress who, Lauren explained in a whisper, hooked on the side when times got rough.

I had no idea at the time what Lauren had meant by "hooked." But I didn't tell her, because I didn't want her to know just how stupid I was.

Wide-eyed, I'd listened to Lauren's matter-of-fact story about her home life as we'd sat together at school during lunch. I'd felt overdressed in my pretty blouse, designer jeans, and new sneakers.

Lauren's typical uniform consisted of ragged jeans and hole-ridden T-shirts. Her mangled, cheap tennis shoes looked like something that someone might have found in a trash bin. Her hair might have been pretty if it hadn't always looked as though it needed to be combed, and washed.

18

I knew I'd never forget that first day, sitting outside at a picnic table at school, listening to Lauren. It was certainly an eye-opening experience for me. I believed that was the day I'd lost my innocence. For the first time, I'd begun to realize that life wasn't a bed of roses for everyone.

"I call him my daddy, but he's not really my daddy," Lauren told me.

When I'd realized she was staring at my roast beef sandwich, I'd offered her half. She'd gobbled it up in two bites, her eyes closed blissfully.

"That was awesome," she murmured around the last mouthful of sandwich. She took the second half without hesitation when I'd pushed it her way.

I'd picked up my apple and begun to nibble on it. I'd wanted to ask if it was the first time she'd tasted roast beef, but I knew that it would have been rude. I didn't want to lose the first real friend I'd ever had by embarrassing her.

"Anyway, Danny, my half brother, is in prison. I have another half brother who lives at home. He's fourteen." She made a face. "Kirk's a punk, though. He's always chasing me and pinching my breasts."

I'd just managed to swallow a shocked gasp before Lauren had heard it. Never in my sheltered life had I heard such talk. I was an only child, but I knew that brothers weren't supposed to touch their sisters' breasts. Just thinking about it made my stomach feel sick.

"He says that it helps them to grow, but I don't believe him," Lauren went on with a shrug. "Got another apple?"

I didn't, so I'd offered her what was left of mine. She'd taken it and eaten it with the same, sad hunger.

Tomorrow, I thought, I'll bring enough for both of us.

That night, as I lay in bed, I'd decided that I was going to share everything with my new best friend. I'd felt ashamed that I had so much, while Lauren had so little.

I'd kept my promise. At lunchtime, I'd shared my food with Lauren, always making sure that I'd brought double. When my parents gave me my weekly allowance, I gave half to Lauren. Lauren spent the weekends at my house, wearing my clothes and pigging out after my parents had gone to bed. She went with me to the movies and shopping with my mother. I didn't really think that Mom liked Lauren much, but she pretended that she did, for my sake. She even bought her a nice outfit for her birthday, and took her to the salon to get her hair cut and styled. My new best friend and I had soon become inseparable.

Summer came, and school let out. For the first time, Lauren had invited me to spend the night with her. I'd asked my mother if I could go, and it was then that I'd found out just how much she'd truly disliked our friendship.

19

"I don't know her family, Brittany," my mother said, shaking her head. "They don't even have a phone, do they?"

I'd immediately jumped to Lauren's defense. "They can't help being poor, Mom. I can't believe that you're acting this way."

But my mother didn't relent. "I'm sorry, Brittany. I have to trust my instincts on this one. She can spend the night here as often as she wants, but you can't go to her house."

When I'd told Lauren, she'd reacted the way that I'd feared she would.

"Your mom's a snob!" Lauren told me. She was trying to act as though she was angry, even though I could tell that she was on the verge of crying. "Just because you guys are rich, she thinks that you're better than me."

"That isn't true," I protested. But, in my heart, I knew that Lauren was right. My mother was a snob. "Don't worry—I'll ask her again."

"Just tell her that you're sleeping over at my house, anyway," Lauren said, daring me with her eyes. "She can't stop you."

In my mind, I knew that she definitely could stop me, but I wasn't going to add to Lauren's hurt feelings by telling her that. I'd never defied my parents, but I wasn't above a little manipulating.

That night at dinner, I'd launched my plan. I had deliberately waited until both my parents were present. Halfway through the meal, my father had noticed that I wasn't talking.

"Brittany, you look like you've lost your best friend," he said.

That was the opening that I'd needed. "I have," I told him mournfully. "Lauren won't speak to me," I went on, keeping my sorrowful gaze on my plate. I was hungry, but I'd pushed my food around as if I had lost my appetite. Later, I'd planned to sneak into the kitchen and eat. "She says that I'm a snob, and that she can't be friends with a snob." I'd flicked a quick, accusing glance at Mom, and I'd felt a sense of shameful satisfaction when I'd noticed that she'd looked guilty.

My father took the bait, as I'd hoped. "What makes her think that you're a snob?" he asked.

I'd sniffed. "Because Mom won't let me spend the night with her. She spends the night with me all the time, but I can't spend the night with her."

"Why not?" he asked.

"Because we don't know her family," my mother insisted firmly. "They don't have a phone. And," she added, "you're only twelve years old."

I'd squeezed out a tear and sniffled some more. "I don't want to go on a date, Mom. I just want to spend the night with my best friend."

"She has a point, honey," my father told Mom.

20

Inside, my heart had leaped joyously. I knew that tone of voice. It meant that he was choosing sides—he was taking my side.

"But, Michael—" Mom protested.

"What's the worst that can happen?" he asked reasonably. "She's just spending the night with her girlfriend. They'll play with dolls, and stay up half the night eating junk food and talking."

The talking part was about the only thing that I could be certain about. I'd already planned on filling my backpack with snacks, but, as far as I knew, Lauren had long since outgrown the doll stage.

My father had put the final twist on the subject by saying: "You've got to trust your own daughter, Lynn."

And so, the stage was set for the worst night of my life, although I hadn't known it at the time. In my naiveté, it had never occurred to me that I would be in any danger by spending the night with Lauren. Sure, she'd told me plenty of horror stories about her home life, but I didn't think I really believed half of what she'd said. I supposed I just couldn't imagine how bad things really were.

The moment I'd stepped across the threshold of Lauren's little shack of a house, I'd felt as if I had stepped into the twilight zone. The living room was about the size of our upstairs bathroom, and the kitchen was no bigger than our linen closet.

There were bugs crawling around everywhere. They were roaches, Lauren had informed me in her customary, matter-of-fact tone. They didn't bite, so she told me that I wasn't supposed to pay any attention to them. I'd felt as if I'd done a wonderful job hiding my revulsion.

Next, we'd hurried past a worn-out recliner where Lauren's stepfather was dozing. His T-shirt was so stained that I couldn't discern the original color, and he'd reeked of beer.

"Don't worry," Lauren whispered, apparently sensing my apprehension. "He'll never know that we're here."

She'd already informed me that her mother would be working until the early hours of the morning—possibly all night. The only other person in the house was her brother, Kirk.

We'd crept down the tiny hall to an even tinier bedroom. Again, I'd silently marveled at the size, comparing it to my walk-in closet at home. The only furniture had consisted of a single bed and a scuffed chest of drawers. The top of the chest was cluttered with makeup, a brush, and several empty soda cans.

At first, I was very uncomfortable, and I'd had to resist the urge to make some excuse and return home. But, by the end of the first hour, I had relaxed. Lauren and I had sat on her tiny bed, experimenting with her makeup. Lauren had insisted on giving me a makeover. I had never worn makeup before, so I was curious.

21

When she was finished, she'd rooted around under the bed, amidst the rubble, and produced a mirror. "Here, take a look," she said, sounding smug.

I'd looked, and I was shocked—and surprised. That was me? Why, I was actually pretty! My eyelashes, enhanced by the mascara, were lovely. Eye shadow had brought out the color of my eyes, and the lipstick had made me look years older.

A low whistle had startled me. I'd swung around to see a boy lounging in the doorway to Lauren's room.

"That's my brother, Kirk," Lauren introduced us, frowning. "Now get lost, Kirk. She's my friend."

I was mesmerized by his magnetic eyes. They'd slowly looked me over. I had just turned twelve a month ago, but I was able to recognized male appreciation when I saw it. Although he spoke to his sister, he never took his gaze from me.

"Well, well, well. Where did you find her?" he murmured sexily.

"Get out, Kirk!" Lauren shouted, her shrill tone making me wince. "Or I'll tell Mom."

He'd given Lauren a narrow-eyed look and shrugged. "Okay. If you don't want any of this wine—" He'd produced a bottle from behind his back. "—then that leaves more for me."

To my surprise, Lauren had leaped from the bed and tried to snatch the bottle from his hands. "Give it to me, Kirk! You promised that the next time you got some, you would share."

I couldn't believe that they were fighting over a bottle of wine. Lauren was thirteen, and Kirk fourteen. Where had they gotten the wine in the first place?

"I'll share," Kirk said softly, "if you'll let me stay." His liquid gaze had darted to me. "I'd like to get know your friend a little better."

I was flattered by his attention, but I was scared, too. Kirk was way out of my league, and I knew it. He was fourteen, going on thirty.

But, still, he was the first boy who had ever looked at me as if I were pretty.

"Okay, but you have to be nice to her," Lauren mumbled grudgingly. "Not like the last time—"

"I don't think that we need to bring that up," Kirk interrupted, giving her a warning look that had aroused my curiosity.

In the end, I'd decided that I was better off not knowing what they'd meant. Surprised my own boldness, I found myself smiling. "I'm Brittany," I told him.

"Hey, Brittany," Kirk said, seating himself next to me on the bed. "Welcome to our castle." He'd laughed at his own joke and taken a drink of the wine straight from the bottle.

Lauren hadn't found his comment to be very funny. "Shut up,

Kirk!" she snapped. "You wouldn't be making fun if you saw Brittany's house. It's a mansion."

It wasn't, but I supposed it had seemed that way to Lauren.

Kirk had offered me the bottle. I froze, aware that both Lauren and Kirk were watching me. I knew that it was a test, and I also knew what I had to do. Reaching out, I'd grabbed the bottle and taken a drink, forcing myself to keep swallowing.

The wine had tasted surprisingly sweet and fruity—not bad at all.

Lauren was next, and we'd passed the bottle around until it was nearly empty. Kirk had asked me about school and my home life. It was almost as if he'd truly cared.

The wine had begun to relax me. My head had felt light, and my mouth fuzzy, when I'd talked—and I'd talked a lot. Kirk had left once, and then, he'd come back with three bottles of beer. The beer hadn't tasted as good as the wine, but I'd tried to enjoy it, anyway, just to prove to them that I wasn't a snob.

Before long, Lauren had fallen asleep. I wasn't the least bit sleepy. I was enjoying the euphoric feeling that the alcohol had given me— and Kirk's attention. He's a nice guy, I thought, smiling happily at him.

"Why don't we go to my room and watch a movie?" Kirk suggested, holding out his hand. "I've got another bottle of wine hidden under my bed."

Since Lauren had fallen asleep, I didn't see the harm, so I'd taken his hand. When I'd stood up, the room had begun to spin. I'd giggled and clutched at Kirk for balance. Leaning on him, I'd made my way down the narrow hall to another room, one that was even smaller than Lauren's. Instead of a bed, there was a single mattress on the floor. I'd given a brief thought to the bugs that I'd seen crawling around earlier. I'd dismissed the idea, though, figuring, in my intoxicated state, that Kirk probably had some way of keeping them out of his room. Otherwise, why would he have put his mattress on the floor?

I'd practically fallen onto the mattress when Kirk had let me go. Through unfocused eyes, I'd watched as he'd put a tape in the VCR, and switched on the small television set.

When I'd seen the naked couple entwined on the screen, my jaw had dropped.

"Don't tell me that you've never seen a porn movie before?" Kirk asked with a hint of scorn. He'd sat next to me on the mattress and offered me a drink from a new bottle of wine.

His scorn, of course, had prompted me to lie. I'd snapped my mouth shut, then snorted. "Of course I have," I told him. I'd taken the bottle and downed a third of it, feeling reckless. The wine was warm, but I didn't care.

23

"Whoa, girl," Kirk said, taking the bottle from my hands. "You'll get sick if you drink it too fast."

Sick? I'd never felt better in my life. I'd started to tell him just how wrong he was, when he'd leaned forward and kissed me.

It was my first kiss, although I would have died rather than have admitted that to Kirk. He'd tasted of the fruity wine and, when he'd thrust his tongue between my lips, I'd somehow managed to hide my shock and kiss him back, hoping that I was doing it right. I didn't think that I could have handled his criticism.

My entire body had begun to tingle. When his hand had crept beneath my blouse, I'd let him touch my developing breasts. I'd gotten my period for the first time a few months earlier, and since then, my breasts had grown considerably.

Behind my closed eyes, I could see a kaleidoscope of colors. When I'd opened them again, I'd had to shut one eye to focus on Kirk's face. That was when I'd realized that I was truly drunk. On occasion, I'd witnessed my parents returning from a party. Based on their loud laughter and stumbling gaits, I had been able to tell that they were drunk, so I'd had some idea of what it was like, to be intoxicated.

"I'd like to see you naked," Kirk whispered, his voice oddly husky as he eased me onto my back.

Somewhere in my alcoholic fog, I'd known that I was doing something wrong—something dangerous—but I couldn't muster the energy to stop Kirk. He was making me feel good, and right then, that was all I'd cared about.

I'd let him undress me. I was foolishly impressed with the tender way he'd kissed me while my clothes had disappeared, one piece at a time.

"You're beautiful," he murmured, gazing at my naked body. Through my alcoholic haze, I'd watched as he'd stood and torn off his jeans and shirt.

For a brief moment, my sanity had returned. He must have read the panic in my eyes, though, because he'd lifted my head and urged me to drink more wine. Afterward, he'd licked the wine from my lips, melting my resistance once again as he'd lowered his naked body onto mine and nudged my knees apart.

I didn't feel much pain when he entered me. I probably had the alcohol to thank for that.

Just as my body had begun to respond to his thrusting rhythm, it was over. With a groan, he'd collapsed on top of me, his breathing heavy and hoarse in my ear.

"You can't tell anybody about this," Kirk muttered breathlessly as he'd rolled away from me. "Unless you want your parents to go ballistic."

24

He needn't have worried. I certainly wasn't about to confide in my parents about that particular night. I knew that if I had, they would have locked me in my bedroom and thrown away the key.

Above me, the water-stained ceiling had swum in and out of view. A sick feeling had washed over me, and I'd moaned.

Kirk was on his feet in an instant. "Don't be sick in my bed. Come on—let's get your clothes on, so I can take you to the bathroom."

He helped me dress and then, he'd half-carried, half-walked me to the tiny bathroom at the end of the hall. Roaches scrambled for cover when Kirk turned on the light. The bathroom had smelled strongly of urine. When I'd fallen to my knees in front of the filthy, rust-stained commode, I'd had no trouble emptying the contents of my stomach into the bowl.

Afterward, I'd closed the lid and rested my forehead on the cool porcelain. The next thing I knew, it was daylight, and someone was pounding on the bathroom door.

To my aching head, it had felt as if they were pounding on me. I'd gotten to my feet and opened the door.

Lauren's stepfather had stood there, his bloodshot eyes gazing balefully at me. "Gotta go," he snarled, shoving me out of his way as if he'd found strange girls in his bathroom on a regular basis.

When I'd looked in on Lauren, she was still asleep. I'd backed out of the room and left the house of horrors, my muddled thoughts focused on my own nice, cheerful bedroom at home.

The long walk home had cleared my head of the cobwebs, but had left it pounding even more unbearably. I'd let myself in, using the spare key we'd always kept under the mat in front of the door. I was hoping that I could get to my room before someone saw me.

Finally, I'd made it, and had fallen onto my own familiar bed, fully clothed. I was twelve years old. I had just lost my virginity, and I had gotten drunk for the first time in my life. I was utterly miserable.

Little did I know that it was just the beginning. . . .

I'd lied to Lauren about what had happened that night. She'd asked me if Kirk had tried anything with me, and I'd simply shook my head. I didn't really blame Kirk for what had happened, although later, I'd realized that he'd probably gotten me drunk on purpose. Still, I was ready to be responsible for my own actions.

It was a mighty noble thought for a twelve-year-old girl to have had—until I'd learned that I was pregnant. By the time I had realized the truth, it was too late to do anything about it.

You see, I was book smart, but when it came to sex and boys, I knew next to nothing. Oh, sure, I knew what having a period meant, and I knew that when a girl started menstruating, she could have a baby. I just hadn't connected the facts to myself. After all, I was only twelve years old. I was still a little girl—at least, by most people's standards.

Marriage and babies were for older women, or so I'd naively believed. Besides, Kirk was only fourteen. I'd never realized that a fourteen-year-old boy was old enough to impregnate someone.

When I'd failed to get my period for three months in a row, I wasn't alarmed. I didn't even consider the possibility of pregnancy. My mother had explained that during the first year, my periods might be irregular. So I'd shrugged it off and attributed my faint nausea to a lingering flu that I knew had been making the rounds at school.

Lauren had finally gotten the ball of suspicion and horror rolling four months after the incident with Kirk. It had happened in gym class, while we were changing. She'd glanced at my chest enviously.

"You're getting boobs that are out of this world, girlfriend," she commented. Then, she'd gone on, a bit maliciously. "And you're putting on weight. Look at your stomach. It's getting round. You must be about to have your period."

"I hope so," I said casually. "I haven't had one in four months." Lauren's face had turned pale as she'd stared at me. I'd frowned, confused at her reaction. "What's the big deal? Mom told me that it wouldn't be regular for a while."

"Four months?" Lauren repeated faintly. She'd glanced wildly around at the group of girls who were changing into their gym clothes. Her fingers had bitten into my arm as she'd yanked me close. "Did you lie to me, Brittany?" she whispered. "Did you lie about you and Kirk? You've got to tell me, if you did."

As it turned out, I didn't have to tell her. She'd seen the guilt on my reddened face.

She'd groaned and closed her eyes. "You're such a fool!" she muttered in a voice so scornful that I drew back. "Don't you get it?" When I'd continued to look dumbfounded, she'd gone on. "You're probably pregnant!"

This time, I'd turned pale as her horrifying words had sunk into my brain. Pregnant? Me? I was only twelve years old! Twelve-year-old girls didn't get pregnant, did they? I couldn't believe it. I refused to believe it.

Fighting tears, I'd jerked my arm free. "You're crazy, Lauren. I'm not pregnant by your stupid brother, or by anybody else," I insisted. "I'm just gaining a little weight, and my periods are messed up."

Lauren had given me a pitying look that had made me want to punch her. She'd folded her arms. "All right," she went on. "Since you know so much, and you don't have anything to worry about, then I guess you won't mind taking a pregnancy test."

I'd tossed my head, furious at Lauren for suggesting something so outrageous. "Fine, I'll take one. You'll see how wrong you are," I snapped.

Right up to the moment of truth, I'd firmly believed that Lauren had lost her mind. Pregnant! Not on your life! I was just a baby myself. In fact, I wasn't even that interested in boys. The incident with Kirk had been just a stupid mistake, and it probably wouldn't have happened at all, if I hadn't been drinking.

That weekend, Lauren had taken my allowance and bought a pregnancy test. She'd told the pharmacist, who knew her, that it was for her mother.

My parents had gone out to eat, so Lauren and I had locked ourselves in my bathroom with the test.

Ten minutes later, I'd opened the door and walked out. My entire body had felt curiously numb, and my vision had begun to darken around the edges.

Lauren had caught me when I'd fainted.

When I'd opened my eyes again, I was lying on my bed. Lauren was sitting next to me. I'd turned my face away from her worldly expression of pity.

"I'm not pregnant," I insisted, staring at the wall.

"Yes, Brittany, you are. You'll have to tell your parents," she said.

Her words had driven me into a belated panic. "I can't!" I was sobbing into my pillow. "They'll kill me. This news will kill them."

"You have to tell them," Lauren repeated firmly. "They're nice people. They won't kill you."

Frantically, I'd grabbed her arm. "I'll just get rid of it, like they do in the movies," I insisted.

But Lauren was shaking her head. "It's too late. By my calculations, you're almost five months pregnant."

I'd known better than to argue. Lauren had always known things that I didn't.

"After you tell them, we won't be friends anymore," she predicted sadly.

Lauren had been right on both counts. When I'd told my parents, they'd thought that I was joking at first.

"I don't find this funny, Brittany," my mother said, glaring at me.

Haltingly, I'd told them what happened with Kirk. Then, I'd described the symptoms that had led to the pregnancy test.

My father had exploded in anger, and Mom had soon followed. For hours, they'd ranted, wavering from disbelief to outright horror. I couldn't remember how long I'd stood there in the living room, waiting for the end of the storm. It had seemed like hours. I remembered getting tired, and wondering if my shaky legs would continue to hold me.

Finally, my mother had really seemed to see me. She must have noticed how frightened I was, and she broke down. She took me in her arms and, together, we'd cried. She'd promised me that everything would be all right—that, one day, I would be able to put the tragic incident behind me, and pretend that it had never happened.

My parents were wonderful. Mom took a personal leave of absence from the firm where she worked so that she could homeschool me until after the baby was born. We'd all agreed that giving up the baby for adoption was the right thing to do. I was too young to raise a child, and my parents had made it clear that one child was all they'd planned for, or wanted. There were plenty of couples, they assured me, who couldn't have children. There were many willing people who would give my child a loving home.

After I'd delivered a seven-pound girl, I wasn't allowed to see her. Everyone had thought that it would be best that way, and I supposed that they were right. For a few hours after I'd had her, my chest had ached, and my arms had felt empty. But, I'd reminded myself that giving her away was proof of my love for her.

Afterward, things returned to normal, and my pregnancy, and the baby, were rarely mentioned again. Despite my parents' warnings, I'd continued to hang around with Lauren at school, even though she was no longer allowed to come home with me. Within a year, though, Lauren had moved away.

My parents' plans for me had continued right on schedule. I'd graduated with flying colors and had gone on to college, and then, law school. I'd put my career before everything else.

When I was twenty-five, I'd met Dave and fallen in love. A year later, we were married in a huge ceremony that cost my father a small fortune. I'd never told Dave about the baby. Perhaps I should have, but the memory was buried so far beneath a mountain of pain that it would have taken me days just to uncover the facts. Dave would have understood, I was certain, but I was unwilling to talk about the child that I'd never seen.

At thirty, I'd looked younger than my age. My daughter would have been eighteen. Does she look like me? I wondered.

"It's your turn, ma'am," a voice told me.

A woman was exiting the bathroom stall, and the girl behind me had alerted me to the fact. I'd gone inside, and was washing my hands at the long row of sinks when I'd heard someone whispering.

"There she is, Jessica. Isn't it freaky how much she looks like you?"

"I don't know, Savannah. She does look like me, kind of."

"Kind of? Come on—she looks just like you, only older. Not much, though. Not old enough to be your mother."

The girl I'd recognized from earlier had sounded disappointed by her observation. Little did she know that inside, I was shaking like a shingle in a hurricane.

Is it possible? I wondered, taking my time as I'd dried my hands.

Jessica's friend had sighed loud enough for me to hear. "Yeah, I guess she's too young. She would have had to have been twelve or thirteen when she had you."

Sweat beaded my upper lip. As calmly as I could, I'd headed for the exit door, keeping my eyes focused straight ahead. I wouldn't look at them, I decided, near hysteria. I didn't want to see if she looked like me. I didn't want to wonder if she was my daughter—the daughter I'd never even held.

The daughter I had given birth to at the age of twelve. My big, shameful secret—the secret that I had been told to forget.

Suddenly, a hand had grabbed my arm. I'd stood there, frozen. I'd thought my heart would pound right through my chest.

"Hey, remember me? I thought that you were my friend, Jessica, because you look just like her." Savannah laughed. "I couldn't resist bringing Jessica to see you. Here, take a look at your twin."

Or, should I take a look at my daughter? I thought.

Slowly, I'd turned, praying that I wouldn't faint. Somehow—I'd never know how—I'd managed a polite smile as I'd focused on Jessica.

It was like looking into a mirror. I couldn't take my eyes from her. I knew then that if she wasn't my daughter, she really was my twin.

"Pretty cool, huh?" Savannah asked, jamming her hands in the back pockets of her jeans and grinning from ear to ear. "Hey, you wouldn't mind telling us how old you are, would you?"

"Thirty." My voice came out hoarsely. I'd continued to stare.

"Oh, well. You see?" Jessica went on with a shrug of her pretty shoulders. "She would have had to have been twelve when she had me. Not my mother."

With great difficulty, I'd inhaled air into my lungs. It had felt as though I were trying to inhale water. "You—" I'd licked my lips, still staring at Jessica's fresh, beautiful face. "You're eighteen?" I finally managed to whisper.

"Yes. I turned eighteen on April the fourth."

At that, my knees had buckled.

"Hey, what's wrong?" Both girls had reached out to catch me by the arms. They'd led me to a bench seat against the bathroom wall, their faces now wearing identical frowns of concern. Several other women had gathered curiously behind Savannah and Jessica.

"Should someone get the manager?" an elderly lady asked, clucking her tongue. "Your sister looks like she's going to pass right out."

"I'll be fine in just a moment," I said faintly. Then, I'd realized what the woman had said. A complete stranger had noticed the resemblance, and she'd assumed that we were sisters.

Jessica shook her head and grinned at me, but the worry had remained in her eyes. "See? Even she sees that we look alike. Are you sure that you weren't adopted?"

She'd sounded so hopeful that I'd nearly cried right then and there. Someone had handed me a damp paper towel and I'd obediently held it to my hot face.

"Were you an only child?" I asked, unable to take my eyes from her. My daughter. Her birth date had confirmed what I had only suspected.

"Yes." Jessica had popped her gum and tilted her head, studying me in much the same way as I'd studied her. I didn't need a mirror to know that our expressions were nearly identical. "How about you?"

"Yes, I was."

"Too bad we aren't sisters, then," Jessica said, sighing. "Well, if you think that you're going to be all right, we'd better get back to our table before my dad comes looking for us."

Her dad. My baby's adoptive father.

Drained and dazed, I'd nodded. They'd walked away, and I'd just sat there and watched. Was I going to let her disappear from my life a second time? I wasn't a child now. I was a grown, married woman—a successful lawyer.

But I knew that if I stopped her, then I would have to tell my husband the entire story, and possibly other people, too. My comfortable, orderly life would undoubtedly change forever.

They were at the door, waiting for a woman and child to pass. Another moment and she would be gone forever.

"Wait!" I heard myself shout. Several people turned to look at me in surprise, including Jessica and her friend, Savannah. I'd read the question in their eyes, and I'd nodded, beckoning them back to me.

A bit warily, they'd obeyed. I'd gripped my hands together to keep them from shaking. My knees had begun to knock, so I'd crossed my legs. There was nothing that I could do about my voice, which wobbled like a warped record when I spoke.

When they were standing in front of me again, I'd looked at Jessica. "If I give you my card, will you promise to call me?" I asked.

Puzzled, she shrugged. "I guess. Any particular reason?"

Instead of answering, I'd rummaged in my purse and found one of my business cards with my name and phone number, and the number of my firm. I'd held it out. "I might have some information about your mother," I said evasively. I just couldn't see myself blurting out the truth in a rest room full of curious women. What I had to say needed to be said in private, and I'd wanted the chance to tell Dave first.

30

Her friend was thrilled. "I knew it, Jessica!" she exclaimed. "She's related to you. Nobody could look that much like you and not be a relative."

Jessica had remained calm, her gaze a little wary, as if she were afraid to hope too much. "Is it true? Are you somehow related to me?"

"We'll talk later." That was all I'd said. As I'd watched her walk away a second time, I'd let the tears fall. I'd sat there for another fifteen minutes or so, thinking and gathering myself together.

Finally, when I was certain that my trembling legs would hold me, I'd gotten to my feet and returned to the table where my husband and my parents waited. I'd decided that I would tell Dave first, alone. Then, I would invite my parents over for coffee and tell them about my decision.

Dave was surprisingly calm when I'd told him that I had become a mother at the age of twelve. His reaction shouldn't have surprised me. After all, one of the things that had attracted me to Dave was his practicality and nonjudgmental attitude toward others.

After I'd finished my story, he'd taken my hand in his and raised it to his lips. His eyes were soft and loving as he'd gazed into my face. "I can't imagine how terrible it was for you to go through something like that as a child."

I'd swallowed a sob. "You don't think I'm awful for giving up my baby?" I asked, needing reassurance.

He'd lifted a disbelieving brow. "At twelve? How could anyone blame you for not keeping her? You were just a child yourself. Of course you did the right thing."

"I wonder if Jessica will understand that," I murmured.

"Of course she will. Just from what you've told me about her, I gather that she's a smart girl."

"Will you be with me when I tell her?" I asked.

Dave smiled. "I wouldn't miss it for the world."

I supposed it was asking too much to have expected my parents to accept my decision without an argument. The next night, I'd invited them over for coffee, telling them that I had something important to discuss with them.

The moment they'd walked in the door, my mother had rushed toward me and hugged me. She'd had tears in her eyes. "You're going to make us grandparents?" she guessed hopefully.

I'd taken a deep breath, knowing that my news would shock them. "You're already grandparents, remember?"

My mother had looked blank for a moment. Finally, realization had dawned in her eyes. The color had drained from her face. "Brittany, surely you're not thinking about tracking her down—" she began.

"I've already found her, Mom," I interrupted gently. I'd poured the coffee and waited until they were seated. "I ran into her at the mall this week. I've scheduled a meeting with her Friday in my office. Dave's going to be there with me." It was a subtle hint that I wanted, and needed, their support.

Surprisingly, my father was the first to offer it. "I've always wondered what happened to her—if she was happy and well." He'd squeezed my mom's hand. "We'll be there, won't we, Lynn?"

As the tears had poured down my mother's face, I'd gone to her, kneeling before her. "Mom, she's eighteen now. I don't expect to just step in and become her mother. I just want her to know why I had to give her up, and maybe get to know her."

After a moment of hesitation, my mother had sighed and put her arms around me. She'd kissed my check. "Okay, sweetheart. If you're sure about this, I'll support you," she promised.

She was late.

My father and Dave had passed each other as they'd paced before the desk in my office. Mom sat as still as a doll in a chair by the window, dressed in a blue skirt and a white blouse, looking every inch the upper-class woman that she was. She had almost completely retired, taking only those cases that interested her.

"She's late," my father announced with a frown.

"She'll be here." I wished I'd felt as confident as I'd sounded. What if she'd changed her mind? What if she had decided that I was some sort of maniac?

And then, suddenly, the intercom on my desk had crackled to life. Abigail, my secretary, had announced a visitor.

"Show her in," I said, willing myself to calm down. Dave and my father had stopped pacing and faced the door. Without looking, I knew that my mother had frozen.

When the door opened, Jessica had walked slowly into the room. She'd glanced at me, then looked from my mother to the men. Her gaze had come back to me.

"You said that you had information about my birth mother," she said in a small voice. She was obviously intimidated by the way that we were all staring at her.

"Come on, have a seat." My hands shook visibly. I'd stuffed them into the pocket of the suit jacket that I wore over my blouse. When Jessica was seated, I'd sat in my chair across from her. I didn't know what to do with my hands, so I'd finally clasped them together to form a steeple.

"I'm your mother," I blurted out.

She gave a nervous laugh. "You're joking, right? You're not old enough." She looked at my mother, obviously noticing the resemblance.

32

It didn't take a genius to see what she was thinking. I shook my head. "She's your grandmother. I gave birth to you when I was twelve years old."

Jessica jerked forward in her chair, her expression one of pure disbelief. "Is this some kind of sick joke?" she demanded, her eyes flashing with anger.

My dad muffled a chuckle. Dave smiled. My mother remained still and silent, her gaze frozen on Jessica. I had a feeling that she was dazed by the remarkable resemblance.

"It's not a joke, Jessica. I'm your mother. I gave birth to you when I was only twelve."

Jessica had closed her eyes a second. Then, she'd shaken her head. "I'm finding this hard to believe. You don't look much older than I do."

"I'm thirty." My throat was aching. Emotionally, I was a wreck, and I was getting worse with each passing moment. My daughter was sitting across from me. It was all too incredible. "Are you ready to hear the story?" I asked.

"Yes," she whispered, her eyes wide with shock. I could tell that the truth was finally sinking in.

Everyone was silent as I'd told her how I'd given birth to her, and then placed her in a good home.

"Unbelievable," she murmured after I'd finished.

"Believe it," I told her, feeling as though a heavy weight had been lifted from my shoulders. "So when I saw you, and realized that you were my daughter, I had to meet you again. I wanted to explain why I gave you up."

Jessica nodded. "I have always wondered. I guess that's a question a lot of adopted children wonder about."

"Did you have a good childhood?" I asked, half-fearfully. I knew that if she'd said that she hadn't, I would never get over the guilt.

"Oh, yes. My parents are wonderful people." Her eyes literally glowed, and I was both glad and envious. "The moment I was old enough to understand, they told me that I was adopted. Naturally, I've been curious ever since." She'd smiled at me. "And now I've met my real mother, who looks more like my sister than my mother."

I'd blushed at the compliment. "I should probably change my hair. Maybe I should dress more conservatively."

Jessica shook her head. "No, don't. I don't mind that you look so young." She'd darted a shy glance at my mother. "So you're my grandmother?"

I'd held my breath, praying that my mother would accept her.

Mom had nodded, then smiled. "Welcome to the family, Jessica. That mean-looking guy over there is your grandfather. But, don't

33

worry—his bark is bigger than his bite."

Soon, we were all trying to talk at once. We were eager to fill Jessica in on the family history, and just as eager to hear everything about her life. Eventually, I grew quiet, content to watch my daughter's flushed face and sparkling eyes, and to listen to her excited, eager voice.

It was a miracle, I decided. A miracle from God himself, bringing us together again. Silently, I thanked Him. I knew that I would be forever grateful.

THE END

MY SPECIAL
PROM DREAM
Will I finally get the
boy I really want?

Sitting outside on the stoop with my teammates from the girls' high school basketball team, I found it difficult to focus on the conversation about our winning season and the latest regional championship. My attention was on Steven Kirkland—and his current girlfriend, Kayla Madison.

The two of them stood under a tree, gazing into each other's eyes dreamily and holding hands. I would have given anything to be in Kayla's shoes. A lot of girls would have, too. Steven was handsome and bright, and just about every other girl—including myself—in our senior class had a crush on him.

Though Steven and I were neighbors and friends, he was clueless about my feelings for him. To him, I was just a girl whom he liked to hone basketball skills with on days when he had nothing else to do. As a preteen, that had been cool. Now that he and I were seniors, it was important for me to have guys—and especially Steven—appreciate the young woman I was struggling to become.

Of course, I loved basketball. But I didn't want to be known as just a jock. I was more than ready to have my first romance, my first kiss, and my first date. I had a bunch of trophies for my skills as a basketball player, but I had no keepsake tokens from old boyfriends, or memories of summer romances the way other girls my age did. When I'd fantasized about dating and romance, Steven's image would always come to mind. My dream was to one day have him look at me the way he looked at Kayla.

When Steven first told me that he was interested in Kayla, I should have told him that I was better for him. He should have been able to look in my eyes and see the affection I held for him. Steven remained clueless about my feelings, though. If I bumped against him accidentally, whenever we played ball, I'd feel faint afterward. I was so affected by his touch.

Maritza, my friend and teammate, tapped me on the shoulder and broke me out of my reverie.

"Lauren, what's the matter with you? You look kind of down today," Maritza said. She noticed that I had been watching Steven and Kayla flirting. "Your neighbor has it bad for Kayla, huh?"

I sighed and looked at my concerned friend. "Yeah, it looks that way. Why haven't I hooked a guy like him?"

"Lauren, you and Steven have been friends forever. Why would you want to hook up with him?" Maritza asked.

I was glad that I hadn't revealed my feelings about Steven. I knew Maritza would never understand. She thought only other girls should be attracted to him. Since I had known him for years, she assumed I thought of him as only a friend—that I wouldn't see in him what every other girl had.

Embarrassed that Maritza suspected I was foolish enough to want Steven, I changed our conversation. "April is almost over and no one has dared to ask me to the prom."

Maritza stood before me and smiled to brighten my sad feelings. "The prom isn't until the third week in May. There's still time. If you don't get a date by then, I'll get my boyfriend's buddy, Kyle, to take you. You know, I told you that he's interested. But he's scared to approach you. He's in awe of you. You're such a good basketball player. Poor Kyle, isn't very athletic. He thinks that you'll reject him because he's not a jock."

Kyle was an okay guy, but he acted so silly. He was always getting in trouble at school for his pranks. He definitely wasn't my ideal prom date. I could just imagine the most special night of my evening being ruined by Kyle acting like a clown and embarrassing me.

"I don't know. I'll get back to you on him," I said, hoping I wouldn't actually have to resort to going to the prom with him. I'd hoped someone other than Kyle would want to escort me.

Maritza eyes brightened. "There's a sale at that store in the mall. You have to come with me. Even though you don't have a date, you should get a dress. It might bring you some luck," she enthused.

"I don't know. I might be wasting money to get a dress without having a date yet," I said.

"You'd better come and get something before all the best dresses get picked over. And—well, if you decide not to go, you can return it and get your money back. But, I'm sure that there's some guy in our classes who wants to take you, but he can't get up the nerve to ask out the most valuable basketball player."

"You really think that a guy wants to take me to the prom?" I asked in a doubtful tone. "I think half these guys don't think I'm a girl. They're so used seeing me wearing sports gear all the time, they can't picture me any other way."

"I think guys can still see that you've got it going on even in baggy jeans and loose shirts. But when you go to the prom, I want to see you wear something that will show off the 'real' you. The one under all the loose clothes. You might even end up being prom queen."

36

Maritza's words made me smile. It would be really nice for me to be seen as being all that, or at least attractive. I wasn't concerned about other people; I wondered what Steve would think seeing me looking feminine. Could I pull it together enough to sway Steven's interest away from his feelings for Kayla?

"Okay, I'll go shopping with you this weekend," I told Maritza. "Someone is bound to ask me. And if they don't, well, I suppose there's . . . there's Kyle," I said, hoping I wouldn't be driven to go with the class prankster.

That Saturday, Maritza and I went to a shop that catered in chic outfits—and great prom dresses. The first person we saw was Steven's girlfriend, Kayla. She was with a friend and was standing in front of a three-way mirror, checking out herself in a gorgeous light blue gown. It made her look even more a like a princess, who deserved to be with a guy like Steven.

Maritza walked up to Kayla and her friend, Erin, to speak. Maritza's locker was next to Kayla's.

"Oh, Kayla, that dress looks great on you. That should be your choice for the prom," she said.

Kayla grinned at Maritza. "I like it, too," she said, turning this way and that, and admiring the image of herself in the gown that fitted her petite body perfectly. "But you should see the silver one I tried on before this. I think I'll get that one, instead. Steven and I can take some amazing pictures with me in that one."

I'd wandered away from Kayla and Erin who went on about details of the prom. I didn't want to hear Kayla go on about Steven and their plans for prom night. I didn't want to depress myself with thoughts of what they'd be doing on the most special night of our high school lives.

I began to browse for a dress for myself. And, for a moment, I wished that there was a store where I could browse for a decent date for that evening, too.

Maritza caught up to me and began to shift through the racks on the other side of me. "Doesn't Kayla make you sick?" she asked, smirking.

I glanced at Maritza skeptically. "The way you two were talking, I thought you and she were girls."

"Please, girlfriend. Kayla doesn't let any girl get too friendly. She's so full of herself. Anyway, she gets on my nerves, sometimes. She knows she's got it going on—clothes, looks, and money. She just needs a personality adjustment."

"And don't forget—the best looking boyfriend," I added, chuckling at the catty way we were talking about Kayla.

"Yeah, that, too," Maritza said. She laughed softly. Then she leaned toward me. "According to gossip around school, I understand Miss Kayla isn't that happy with Steven."

I stared at Maritza with interest. "Not happy with Steven!" I exclaimed. "What is there not to be happy about him?"

"Kayla is used to getting whatever she wants. I understand that she has been going with Steven only to make that football player named Martin jealous. The two of them dated for a while, but they stopped dating all of sudden. I understand Martin doesn't want to be tied down to one girl. I think Kayla felt that if he saw her all over Steven, he'd realize that she is the one he needs as his only girl."

"Oh, no, that's a shame. Steven doesn't deserve to be used that way," I said. "I should tell him about this."

"No!" Maritza said. "Don't go running and telling him. I'm telling you this confidentially. Someone else made me promise not to tell. If you talk, then that person will know that I opened my mouth and won't tell me anything else—ever."

"Well, you know, Steven and I are neighbors and friends. I would want him to tell me if someone were using me," I said.

"If I were you, I would stay out of it. I've seen the way that Steven looks at Kayla. The friendship you have with him might be over if you bring him that kind of news. Let it be. Promise me that you won't say anything," she implored.

I hesitated, thinking I should tell Steven about Kayla's false feelings for him. But I didn't want to betray Maritza's friendship, either. "I won't say anything," I agreed reluctantly.

"Good," Maritza said. "I know that you and Steven are friends, but we girls have to stick together. All I can say is that we can stand back and see how this drama plays out among Steven, Kayla, and Martin."

Our conversation about Steven's problem soon ended. Maritza pulled out a red gown and held it against herself to look in the mirror.

"How do you like this for me?" she asked.

"I like that color for you," I said, eyeing it carefully. "If I was Kayla, I would feel like the luckiest girl in the world to have him as my boyfriend. If she didn't care about him in the beginning, she probably does now."

"You're still worried about Steven? Look, the word is that Kayla is tired of having to sit at home on most Fridays and Saturdays because Steven works at the grocery store. People like Martin and her don't know anything about having to work. They come from homes where their parents are able to give them everything they want."

"Yeah, you're right," I said. I thought about the brand-new flashy car that Martin's parents had given him when he turned eighteen, and the designer clothes Kayla always wore. I sighed before continuing.

"It's a shame that Kayla is cheating on Steven. He and I work the same shift at the grocery store. Whenever he has a break, he rushes to the phone to call her. She just doesn't know how lucky she is."

"Well, I'm done talking about Kayla and her love life. I'm going to try on this dress. I have a social life of my own to worry about. You'd better find something for yourself," Maritza advised, hustling toward the dressing room with the red gown.

Pushing thoughts of Steven's dilemma out of my mind, I went through the gowns before me, trying to decide what would make me look like a princess for an evening. Unlike Kayla, I didn't have a soft, curvy body. My body was well toned and firm and more boyish. Then my interest fell on a hot pink dress with thin straps. I held it to me and liked the way the color complemented me. I decided to try it on to see how it would hang on me.

In the dressing room, the moment I slipped on the dress made of satin, I no longer felt like the tomboy jock. Standing before the mirror, I admired the way the gown clung to me and made me look more feminine and prettier than I imagined. Fascinated with my appearance, I unbraided my hair and ran my fingers through it. I smiled at my transformation from jock into a prom queen.

Suddenly, I heard Maritza calling out my name in the corridor of the dressing room. I responded by peeking out and waving her to me.

When Maritza entered the room, wearing her selection of gown, she grinned. "Oh, my goodness, Lauren, you look amazing! It's a shame you've been dressing like a boy." Her eyes were wide with admiration. "You have to get this. This is you!"

I agreed with her. Even though I didn't have a date yet, I wasn't going to give up hope. "I am going to buy it, Maritza. It's worth the price because it makes me feel special. I have a feeling it will be my lucky charm. Now I'm sure to get a delicious date."

"Now you're talking!" Maritza said. "The prom is going to be a night neither of us will ever forget."

Feeling giddy, I agreed with my friend's positive outlook. Carefully slipping out of the gown and returning it to the rack, I ran my hand down the length of it as though it held enchanting powers like Cinderella's glass slipper. It had brought her and her prince together. Smiling at my dreams, I had a feeling that something wonderful was going to happen to me within the next few weeks.

A few days after we'd seen Kayla at the store, things became dramatic around school. Word got back to Steven about Kayla seeing Martin, the football player, behind his back. According to the rumors, one of Martin's friends had taken pleasure in telling Steven of Kayla's unfaithfulness in the library. The guy had said other things about Kayla and called Steven some names. They'd had a fight right in the library.

After the fight broke up, Steven rushed to Kayla with what he had heard. She hadn't denied her feelings for Martin. She'd even told him that she hadn't wanted to be his girl. She hated the idea that he had to work all the time, and that he hadn't the time or money to take her to the kind of places Martin could take her to as often as she wanted.

When Maritza sought me out after school to relate all of this to me, I was hurt for the way that Steven had been humiliated. I worried about Steven and considered talking to him. I knew that he needed my friendship more than ever. Then I'd decided just to leave him alone. I figured he might be too ashamed to admit the one girl he loved had made a fool of him. I hoped he would show up at work that evening. Maybe when we took our break, I would be able to ease into a conversation about his awful relationship.

By the time that I'd arrived for work at the grocery store, I was pleased to find Steven working the cash register on the express line. However, I took one look at him and could tell that he was miserable. He didn't smile or chat the way he normally did when he waited on customers. Nor did he kid around with the other employees. He kept his head down and kept as busy as he could with the odd jobs that we did when there were no customers to ring.

During our break in the employees' lounge, Steven sat in the back facing the wall. He seemed as though he didn't want anyone to talk to him. I wasn't going to allow him to shut me out. He was hurting, and I'd wanted to offer my shoulder to him. After all, we were friends. Taking a seat at the table with Steven, he gave me a grim look.

"I bet you heard what happened between Kayla and me, and you're waiting to hear all the juicy details to take back to your friends," he said in cold tone.

"You know I'm not like that. Yes, I heard, and I'm really sorry. You don't deserve to be treated the way you were," I told him.

He sighed and met my gaze shyly. "I really liked Kayla." He folded his arms on the table and grew pensive before continuing. "I'm–I'm going to be okay. I'm going to be just fine," he said as though he were trying to convince himself.

I touched him on his shoulder and wished that I could convince that he would be fine. "You will. I'm here for you. I hope you think of me as a friend—someone that you can always count on."

He swung his gaze to meet my mine and squeezed my nose playfully, offering me a weak smile. "That means a lot to me, Lauren. Thanks."

Steven picked up his sandwich, took a bite, and chewed it as though he didn't like what he tasted. Then he rewrapped it, and set it aside. He slumped in his seat. "Looks like I'm dateless for the prom." He looked down. "I was really looking forward to it. I've been saving

40

my money so the night could be great for me–and, uh–well, you know who."

My heart lifted a bit. Then I'd made my admission. "I don't have a date, either. I went out and bought a gown, but I haven't been asked to go yet." I chuckled nervously. "I still have my receipt, so I guess I'll just get my money back."

He smiled weakly. "C'mon, someone will come through and ask you. I can't believe no one has asked you to the prom, though. I don't know what's wrong with the guys around school. They are always saying that you're a nice person, and that they'd like to get to know you. I guess they are intimidated by you because you're considered one of the best athletes in school."

I shrugged, flattered by what he had said. Why can't the two of us go to the prom together? I thought.

At last, I'd noticed a flicker of excitement in Steven's sad eyes. "Would you mind going to prom with a loser like me?"

My heart had thumped in my chest so hard I was sure Steven could hear it. "You're far from a loser. And, yes, I would like to be your date." I gave him my best smile.

Steven beamed. "Hey, we'll probably have a great time. We're friends, so we can relax and just have fun."

"Exactly," I agreed quickly.

Though Steven saw the situation as a solution to his dateless prom evening, I viewed it as a miracle that would turn one of my long-time fantasies into a reality. It would also help to soothe his tarnished pride. Yet, I wished the date could have been made because he'd really wanted to take me. I'd hoped that all that would change that night.

The next few days at school were exciting for me. I was pleased about the way that Steven let everyone at school know how he was taking me to the prom. Suddenly, my classmates looked at me differently. I was no longer just the girl who was a good basketball player, but I was the girl that Steven Kirkland had chosen to take as his date to the prom.

Kayla's flirtations had backfired. The secret romance she had with Martin wasn't so wonderful anymore. According to Maritza, who kept her finger on the pulse of gossip in school, she had learned that Martin had his sights on a new girl who had transferred to our school. Unhappy with Martin, Kayla had gone to Steven and attempted to make up with him.

The situation made me nervous. Though Steven said that he was through with her, I knew his feelings for her were still strong. I knew that people didn't turn love on and off like a light switch. I lived in fear of Steven coming to me at the last minute and telling me that he and Kayla had made up and that he would rather attend the prom with her.

And since I was a friend, I would probably be understanding and not make him feel bad about the last-minute change of plans.

But, thankfully, my negative thoughts didn't come true. I put all thoughts of the scheming Kayla out of my mind and focused on my big evening with Steven. I believed with everything in my heart and soul that one evening with him would make him see me in a different light. I hoped that once he saw me in my prom dress, he would stop thinking of me as one of the guys. On our prom night, I wanted him to look in my eyes and see the hidden love that I'd been harboring for him for so long.

The night of the prom was the most thrilling of my life. I knew I would never forget the way Steven's face had held a look of awe when he glimpsed me in my pink gown with my hair worn loose and framing my face.

Steven's face twisted in a smile as though I had revealed a secret to him. Looking elegant in his black tuxedo, he'd fitted a lovely corsage of deep pink roses on my wrist. He'd held my hand tightly while gazing in my eyes. The admiration was clear in his expression.

"Looks as though I've lost my best basketball partner," he said softly. "You are beautiful, Lauren."

I held on to his hand and smiled warmly at him. "Thanks. You don't look half bad yourself."

He winked at me. "Let's go and party!" He held onto my hand and led me out of the house enthusiastically toward his car, which he had polished brightly for the event.

Arriving at the hotel ballroom on Steven's arm, I'd noticed the way the guys had eyed me the way they did the prettier girls at school. Several of them came over to speak to us and made sure to tell me how pretty I looked. They asked that I save a dance for them. My spirits and confidence soared several levels.

"Hmm. . . it looks as though you're turning into the main attraction," Steven said, holding on to my hand. "With you looking as pretty as a model, I have a feeling that I won't have you to myself. The guys are checking you out. They can't wait for their chance to dance or talk to you. They look like hungry vultures," he teased.

Steven's words made my heart swell with joy. I was amazed, yet very pleased, by the attention. It truly felt as though the night was mine. The night was going to be both interesting and fun, I realized.

I was glad that Steven and I had come as two friends who just wanted to take part in one of their class's major events. Suddenly, I didn't want to spend the entire evening with Steven. I wanted to be able to socialize with anyone who wanted to talk to me. Coming to the prom made me feel as though I had become the person that I'd always wanted to be. I felt like I was a butterfly who had come out of her cocoon and was spreading its wings for the first time.

Although Steven and I had agreed to come to the dance as friends, I had a feeling he was becoming annoyed by the constant flow of guys. They approached me throughout the evening, asking for a dance or a chance to take a photo with me. Whenever I was on the dance floor, I saw him, sitting at our table, sipping punch as though he wished the evening were over.

When the band broke into a slow song, Steven appeared out of nowhere and stepped in front of a guy who had come to ask me to dance.

"This one is mine, man," he told the guy, sliding his arm around my waist and falling into the tempo of the song. "I know we said we were coming as friends, but I had no idea you'd desert me the entire evening. What a way to treat a friend!" He chuckled.

"You're free to dance with whomever you want." I reminded him of our friendship agreement for the evening.

"I'm fine. I came so that I could at least have a memory of a prom. It doesn't matter how much I dance as long as you give me a chance to dance a few times with you–the dancing queen of the evening," he said.

"I'm having the time of my life. I've had several guys to ask me out," I murmured, no longer wanting to capture solely his attention. "Can you believe what a gown and a little makeup can do? Before tonight, the only reason a guy wanted to see me was to play basketball," I told my friend, Steven who had considered me only his friend all those years.

Steven stared at me with a twinkle in his eyes. "I'm glad you're having such a good time. But you have to save some dances and time for me. After all, I brought you to here," he reminded me. Then he'd pulled me closer to him, so we could continue our slow dance.

While I danced with Steven, I thought of how much fun I'd had during the evening with the other guys. I realized that I had been attracted to Steven for so long, because he was one of the few guys I'd felt comfortable talking to about being self-conscious for being an athlete. Although I was glad that Steven had escorted me the prom, I was beginning to feel that I'd wasted too much interest on him only. But with my studies, basketball practice, and the games, I had no time to socialize or think about any other guys than Steven who lived nearby.

Though I was pleased that Steven had asked me, deep down inside I suspected he came with me, hoping he could show off for Kayla. He had too much pride to let her know how hurt he was. Later, he had admitted it to me confidentially.

The highlight of the evening for me came when we took our formal pictures. I was thrilled that I would have pictures of myself, looking glamorous and so happy, from all the attention I had received. I had come to the prom, hoping for a romance with Steven. Yet, in the process, the prom became to mean much more to me. I knew it was the night I became a confident young woman who didn't really need a special guy to make her life complete.

By the time Steven and I had made our way through the long line to take our pictures, the band had taken an intermission. I excused myself and headed for the rest room, hoping I could run into Maritza whom I hadn't been able to talk to all evening.

Sure enough, I'd found my friend there, touching up her fancy hairdo. I'd eased up behind her.

"I knew I'd find you here. You just can't stay out of a mirror, can you?" I teased her.

Maritza grinned and turned and hugged me. "Lauren, I'm so happy for you. Every time I caught a glimpse of you, you've been dancing with a different guy. Everybody is talking about how great you look. And that dress, your hair—everything looks perfect. You look better than our homecoming queen," she enthused.

I grinned harder at her compliment. "I'm having the best time. I wish this night would never end."

"Yeah, I know what you mean. Just think, this is the last time we'll have a chance to party with all of our classmates this way. I can't believe how friendly and relaxed everyone is with each other. There are no little cliques. It's a shame it took us four years to feel this way."

"You're right," I agreed. "It feels like there is magic in the air."

Maritza leaned closer to me. "How do you like Steven as your date? Though you never admitted it to me, I always felt you had special feelings for him."

"I had a crush on him. I thought I'd done a good job of hiding it from you." I giggled. "But I think I'm over that now. He's nice and all, but he's still going through this emotional stuff with Kayla. I still want to be his friend, but I think I'd like to date and just have fun, like tonight. I've made two dates tonight. Can you believe that? I tell you, I'm so glad I chose this dress. It's done wonders for my social life." I laughed, twirling playfully.

Maritza laughed at my action and grabbed me by the wrist to calm me down. "Listen, Kayla and her date, Martin, showed up late. The two of them sure didn't look like they were in the party mood. Someone told me Martin was slipping off to drink from a flask he'd hidden in his coat. My table is near Kayla's and Martin's and they've done more bickering than dancing and mingling. I caught Kayla staring at Steven as though she wished she was with him."

"I can imagine she probably wants him back. Steven is a good guy."

I was able to speak without any envy. Since I'd been with Steven, I believed it would be best for us to be just friends.

"It's a shame she ruined the good thing she had with him." I ran a brush through my hair and touched up my makeup.

"Come on, let's get back to the ballroom. This night is going to be over soon." I urged Maritza out of the rest room by taking her by the hand.

Returning to the ballroom, I didn't see Steven at our table. Before I could take a seat, Phillip, who was president of the student council, came up to me and asked me for a dance. I gladly accepted his invitation. A slow dance gave Phillip and me a chance to talk. He let me know that I looked great and mentioned that there was no one special in his life. The girl he had brought to the prom was just a friend. He hinted at giving me a call and maybe going out and getting to know each other better.

Phillip wasn't half bad looking, and he had a real nice personality. His date was one I was going to make a priority over the others. I smiled warmly and told him to call me, and that I'd be interested in going out with him.

In the middle of my dance with Phillip, I heard a rumbling noise across the ballroom. Several of the chaperones hustled toward the confusion as well as curious onlookers. I went to see what was going on. As I got closer to the action, I was stunned to see Steven and Martin, fighting. Kayla stood to the side, quivering and crying, with her gorgeous gown ripped in the front. One of the guys had placed his jacket around Kayla, to cover her.

Suddenly two hotel security guards appeared and hauled Steven and Martin out of the ballroom. Kayla was taken away by one of the female chaperones.

Maritza rushed up to me and hooked her arm with mine. "Are you okay, Lauren? I know you are disgusted by all of this. What in the world is going on with Steven?"

I shook my head and looked at Maritza. "Steven and Martin must have had words over Kayla. Despite the way she cheated on him, Steven isn't over her. The fight made that obvious."

"Oh, I'm sorry," Maritza said.

"No, don't feel sorry for me. I'm fine. I just hope Steven is okay, and hasn't gotten himself in any serious trouble for fighting tonight. His behavior could keep him from participating in our graduation ceremony."

I worried for him for that reason only. I excused myself and went out in the hall to talk to one of the chaperones about Steven. After all, I was a friend who really cared.

After what seemed like forever, Steven appeared, looking disheveled and sporting a swollen bottom lip.

I rushed up to him. "What in the world happened Steven? Are you all right?" I took his hand to comfort him.

Steven placed his back against the wall, touched his swollen lip, and winced. Then he proceeded with his story.

"When you left me for the ladies' room, I started making the rounds in the ballroom, talking to people I hadn't had a chance to speak to during the course of the evening.

Then I noticed Martin had Kayla cornered, and that she was tearful. He was making them a spectacle by kissing and fondling her as though she was cheap. Of course, she struggled with him to keep him in line. Then he became loud and verbally abusive. As she tried to get away from him, he held onto her and called her names. She broke away from him, but he caught her, and ripped her dress.

Seeing Kayla treated that way angered me. I rushed up to Martin and tried my best to knock him off his feet. He cursed me but I told him to shut up. I grabbed Kayla by the hand to get her away from him. Then he punched me and we started fighting. When I did that, he walked up to me and punched me hard. And from there, he and I went at it punch for punch."

In the past, I probably would have been upset and jealous. But I wasn't bothered by the way Steven had fought to protect Kayla. "Did you get in any trouble?" I asked.

"No, I didn't. Martin did, though, for being drunk and for what he did to Kayla. Of course, he can't stay at the prom. I don't think he's going to be allowed to participate in the graduation ceremony, and he's getting suspended from school." He shrugged indifferently.

"Where's Kayla now?" I asked.

"She's still with the chaperone. I think they're going to call her parents to pick her up," he said, looking worried.

I could tell he was concerned. "If you like, we can leave now. She can get a ride with us and you can see her home safely."

A look of relief flooded his face. "You wouldn't mind?"

I was over my infatuation with him. "No, I wouldn't. Friends are supposed to help friends."

Steven leaned toward me and embraced me and whispered in my ear. "You're the greatest." Then he rushed off to get Kayla.

Returning to the ballroom, Maritza came up to me. "Lauren, I heard about that mess over Kayla. I bet she's gloating over having two guys fighting over her. It looks to me like she's going to ruin your evening."

I sighed with frustration. "I don't want to believe that. But Steven and I are leaving, so we can take Kayla home. Her date was ordered to leave the premises."

Looking disappointed, Maritza said: "You shouldn't leave yet. A lot

46

of people are talking about voting for you as the prom queen."

I gave her a look of amazement. "You can't be serious. I'm not the kind of girl who'd win anything like that."

Maritza was excited. "Well, a lot of people have been impressed with you. You've really represented the girls' basketball team. You've shown everyone that we can be as charming and pretty as all the other girls in school. The other girls said that we couldn't be feminine or charming the way you have been all evening. Stay. My date and I will give you a ride home."

"I couldn't impose on you that way this evening."

I glanced and saw Steven with a comforting arm around Kayla. The comforting expression on his face told me that he still cared for her. In that instant, I decided I wasn't going to leave the prom. I turned to Maritza.

"On second thought, I think I will stay. This evening is too important to miss one moment," I told Maritza. "Excuse me a minute. Will you do me a favor and get my things from the table where Steven and I were sitting?" I wanted to have a moment alone with my date, my friend Steven without a curious Maritza standing over my shoulder.

As I strolled up to Steven, he smiled politely. "We're ready to go," he said.

Kayla wouldn't look at me. She murmured: "Thanks for being so understanding, Lauren. I really appreciate this."

"Listen, I've decided to stay to the prom," I announced to them.

Kayla turned and gave Steven an apologetic look. "I didn't want to ruin your date," she whined not sounding very sincere.

"Lauren, let me see Kayla home. I can come back," he said, searching my face.

I looked at Steven. "No, you go on with Kayla. She needs you, and I'll be fine. I've made arrangements to spend the rest of the evening with my friend and her date."

Steven looked at me then Kayla as if he didn't know what to do.

"Steven, take Kayla home. We'll talk tomorrow, and I'll fill you in on what you missed out on." I touched Kayla on the shoulder. "I'm really sorry for what happened." Then I walked away from them toward the ballroom.

As soon as I entered the ballroom, Maritza dashed for me, wearing a broad grin. "Where have you been? They've been calling your name. You've won! You're prom queen, Lauren!" She threw her arms around me, hugged tightly, and then shoved me in the direction of the platform where, Phillip, the class president, had already been crowned prom king stood, waiting for me. As I ascended the steps, he reached for my hand and someone set a crown on my head. Then we walked to the center of the platform. People were whistling and applauding his or her approval.

When Phillip kissed me on the cheek and said congratulations, I hugged him tightly and uttered the same sentiment.

Phillip escorted me down on the ballroom floor where he and I had the floor to ourselves to dance as the royalty of the prom. In Phillip's arms, I felt as though I was really a princess.

That night had changed my life. It would be a night I'd never forget.

THE END

BABIES HAVING BABIES
We had to grow up fast for our son

It was going to be a hot one. Already, I was damp with perspiration as I rested against Guthrie. We'd thrown off the top of our sleeping bag during the night, exposing us to anyone wandering through the public campground, but I didn't care. During my five months with Guthrie, I'd stopped caring about a lot of things like modesty, money, newspapers, and a roof over my head.

Instead, Guthrie taught me to put value in the truly important things in life—like the way a butterfly looks emerging from its cocoon and the smell of sun on the earth in the middle of a hot afternoon.

There was only one thing Guthrie hadn't taught me:

How to get over loving him.

I didn't want to look at him that last time because it was so hard. I nearly gave in and dropped my pounding head to his broad chest, but the time for that was already long gone. No more would we walk hand in hand along a coastal highway or eat lunch together beneath the shade of a California redwood because that day, I was leaving him.

Quickly, my feet making no sound, I reached for the bundle that was all I owned in the world. My one blouse had only two buttons left and I had to tie it in front to cover myself. Guthrie's old jeans were the only thing of his I would take with me because mine no longer fit.

That's why, my darling, I told him wordlessly. That's why I'm leaving you and the sunlight you carry in your beautiful, deep, brown eyes. You're the incredible creature you are because you're free. And what I carry inside of my body means the end of your freedom. I can't bear for that to happen to you, Guthrie.

Jovan and Dave had made my decision for me the night before. When our traveling companions thought I was asleep and the beers had relaxed them, Jovan asked the question that shattered any illusions I had that my secret still belonged to me alone.

"Hey, dude—how much longer is Sienna going to be able to keep up?" he asked.

"Keep up? What do you mean?" Guthrie's voice was low as usual and I had to strain to hear him over the sounds of a camper pulling into one of the nearby camping spots.

"I'm talking about the baby, man. She's gonna need medical care or something soon, isn't she?"

"What baby?"

Dave laughed. "Come on, man! Don't tell me you two thought you could keep that from us! Look, man—we don't care. If Sienna wants to hump a kid all over that's all right with us, but she's not going to want to give birth just anywhere, right?"

"You aren't making sense!" Guthrie snapped. "Sienna's on the Pill."

"Then where did that potbelly come from and why's she so pooped all the time?"

I could tell Guthrie was looking my way suddenly, but I kept my eyes closed and lay still as death in the sleeping bag. "You're imagining things, man. Look—she's five feet tall, not six feet like us. She's got to take twice as many steps as we do. And so what if she's put on a little weight? She can use it. Jeez, don't you think I'd know if she was pregnant?"

"Okay, okay. Forget I said anything, man." Jovan sighed.

"You bet I will." Guthrie still sounded upset. "After all, Sienna knew the deal when she asked to come along: No strings for any of us."

"You got that right, man," Dave said. "Responsibility's for the idiots in suits. This is our time in life to be free, to really live, man."

"Amen," Guthrie echoed. "No bills or taxes. What more could we ask for?"

It was quiet for a moment and then they started talking about whether we should sign up with a temporary agency or head up into Oregon as long as the weather held. Not that it mattered to me; I already knew that I wasn't going to be a part of their world anymore.

As I lifted my pack to my shoulders I could smell bacon frying somewhere in the campground. We'd spent three perfect days there, fishing and going on nature hikes and buying groceries with the last of the money we'd made working at a county fair. Even if Guthrie hadn't been with me I would've loved the quiet surroundings. After the way I grew up, my soul needed time to listen to the music made by quails and crows—time to watch a doe and her fawn in a quiet, misty meadow.

But that time was over for me now. No longer would I walk hand in hand with the only man I'd ever loved. His child was growing inside of me, but that child could only represent a trap for his free spirit. I couldn't do that to him after all of the tenderness he'd given me for five precious months; the way I looked at it, the least I could do was to leave him free to go on searching for whatever his restless heart wanted from life.

Still, I longed to kneel one more time—to take the memory of Guthrie's kiss with me, feel his scraggly beard against my lips. But I knew he would awaken, reach for me, and re-envelop me in the love

50

he offered so freely and openly. Instead, I turned my back on my man and walked to the edge of the campground.

I never looked back.

The highway was almost deserted that time of the morning, but I didn't care because I needed solitude unbroken by the sound of tires on pavement. There was a crazy, half-sick sound to the beating of my heart that grew and enveloped me. Soon the sound pressed against my eyes, breaking through my defenses. The road blurred ahead of me as I walked along.

Good-bye, Guthrie. Good-bye to the crazy love we shared when the world was sunshine without shadows. Yes, my darling, I always understood the unwritten contract between us: No ties, no commitments—each of us with our separate lives, coming together only for as long as our hearts sang the same tune. . . .

Well, my heart was singing another song now. I didn't comprehend it fully then, but I knew that Guthrie would want no part of it.

"Marriage, mortgages, babies—they're for people who know what they want out of life, Sienna," he'd told me more than once. "I don't yet know what I want—maybe I never will. But I'm not going to subject anyone to my indecision. So whenever you want to break away, I won't stop you. All I ask is that you give me the same respect."

I understood his code. From the day I walked out of that McDonald's where I'd been flipping burgers and into his arms I knew what I was getting into. We'd known each other less than a week then, but he offered me love and warmth and a brilliant day and at the time, that was all I thought I would ever need—could ever want. At the time, I wanted escape from my half-life, and that brown-eyed wanderer offered me the answer.

Unfortunately, I was stupid enough to think that buying food instead of birth control pills one month wouldn't hurt. Now it was my problem, not Guthrie's.

By nine o'clock my stomach was growling and the back of my blouse felt like I'd been swimming in a heated pool. I think I could've stood that and my swollen ankles, but my pounding head and aching heart seemed to take up every inch of my exhausted body; I knew I had to rest.

I was sitting on the side of the road, trying to press my throbbing veins back into my temples, when a highway patrol car pulled up beside me.

"You okay?" the young officer asked.

I wanted to nod—that's the standard thing to do, isn't it? But I couldn't quite pull it off. Instead, I stared inside his patrol car, vaguely fascinated by the mounted rifle I glimpsed inside behind his head.

One bullet, I thought, and nothing would ever hurt again. . . .

"It's going to get pretty hot today," he went on. "Maybe you should find someplace to stay for the day."

"I don't have any place."

He smiled faintly. "That's what I thought. How would you like a lift into town?"

I thought about his offer. It seemed so hard to make a decision right then, but finally I pulled myself to my feet. He didn't have much to say during the twenty-mile trip to the small tourist trap, but from time to time I could feel his eyes on me.

No wonder, I thought. He must see hundreds of hikers this time of year, but how many girls walking alone, looking completely wrung out like I do?

"There's a flophouse on the west side of town," he said as we reached the city limits, "but I think the Salvation Army might be a better choice for you. Safer, at least."

"Anything," I whispered. For five months Guthrie had taken care of finding a soft stretch of ground for our sleeping bags.

I no longer knew how to think of myself as someone separate from him.

The shelter was a stark, white building with a small lawn set off the highway about twenty yards. The woman I was introduced to in the clean-smelling lobby started asking me questions so fast that I almost turned and ran. Only, I didn't have anywhere else to go, did I?

"Come on, Flo—give the girl a break," the patrolman interrupted. "Why don't you at least feed her first?"

I was grateful for his suggestion—make that grateful for anything. I don't know why, but I couldn't put anything together right then. I probably would've gone on standing for hours in that room with the blaring TV if he hadn't taken my arm and led me over to a couch.

"You okay?" he asked me again.

That time I managed a nod, one I'm sure he didn't believe. I wished I could find a way of thanking him for looking after me, but suddenly it seemed as though I didn't even know how to put words together anymore.

I managed to eat the olive loaf sandwich Flo gave me, but when she started trying to find out about me again, I shut her out, thinking through the burn in my head, Not now. Please. I can't bear it now. Later. Give me time. Give me a chance.

But I didn't get much time or much of a chance, because Flo didn't give up. "Look, honey," she said, sitting down on the couch beside me. "I want you to know something right from the first: You're not in trouble, see? There's no law against going for a hike. But when I see a young gal wandering around alone with no way to support herself, well, you can guess what runs through my mind."

52

I stared at her, afraid of what she was going to say next.

"I've seen a lot of runaways since I took this job, honey, and you've got the symptoms written all over you." She smiled kindly, her soft, faded, blue eyes crinkling at the corners as she cocked her head to one side and considered me. "Am I right?"

I knew she was waiting for some kind of answer from me, but I simply couldn't.

"Okay," she said, gripping my arm. "Let's take it one step at a time, then. How old are you, honey? I can dig for the information, but you don't want to make my job any harder than it is, do you? What are you—seventeen?"

"Eighteen," I answered, my voice sounding rusty. Seventeen when I left home, but a woman now—a young woman with a baby growing inside of her.

"Well, that gets you in under the wire." She smiled. "You're not considered a juvenile, is what I mean. No one's going to pack you back home. Just the same, I'm not going to pat you on the shoulder and let you go on your way. I'd lose too much sleep and you don't want to be picked up for being a vagrant, do you, now?"

I shook my head.

"What do you want, then?"

Her question took me by surprise. What I wanted was Guthrie's warm body beside me; I wanted to listen to his soft voice whispering words of love in my ear. But that was all over now.

"I—I guess I need a job."

"Good thinking. What kind of work have you done?"

I thought back to the one kind of real job I'd had: working at McDonald's. I decided I wasn't much good at working around a lot of people in a fast-paced environment. "I—I really haven't done much," I stammered. "I—I babysat a lot—when I was in high school."

"You graduate?"

I shook my head. Not that I didn't want to, but my mother was fed up with supporting me and she wanted me out of the way so a certain jerk would marry her.

"Too bad," Flo said, cutting into my thoughts. "I'll see if I can find something for you, but in the meantime, I suggest you get on over to the employment office if you don't intend on going home." She wrote down the address of the employment office on a slip of paper and handed it to me. "Think it over," she said. "I'll even lend you a quarter for the phone if you decide to go back to your family."

Later that afternoon I went to the employment place and filled out their forms. There were some openings at the local fast-food joints, but when the manager at Hotdog Heaven learned that I didn't have anyplace to stay, he told me he had something else that might work for me: a live-in housekeeping job at a small nursing home.

"The pay's not great," he said, "but they'll furnish you with all your meals and a room with a private bath."

Almost before I had time to think about it he was giving me directions to the place. I couldn't afford bus fare and by the time I walked the mile there I was just about ready to drop.

"You sure you're strong enough to push a mop?" the heavyset woman in white asked me. "I've had so many housekeepers this past year that I'm desperate to take on anyone, but I don't want to pay someone who can't work."

I assured her that it was just the heat. That, I thought glumly, and the big hole in my heart that Guthrie used to fill. "I'll be fine, ma'am, honest." I took a deep breath. "But there's something I feel I have to tell you . . . I'm pregnant."

She looked at me for a long time before saying anything. "I'll level with you, then. I don't really want to hire you, but I'm in a bind. It isn't because you're not married, which I gather is the story. That's your business and hardly unique anymore. But I've seen girls like you before. They're sometimes such emotional messes that they can't do anything."

"I promise I'll keep my feelings to myself." I knew I was begging, but I was desperate. I knew I had to have someplace to stay if I were to go on living; I certainly couldn't just go on walking without any money. "I can do the job, ma'am; I know I can."

Finally she told me I was hired; then she went on to tell me about the job. It was mostly a matter of keeping the residents' rooms clean and keeping an eye on the elderly residents. I wasn't responsible for much beyond that, but as she said, "If one of them feels like talking and you've got a minute, they'll love you for listening."

How easy she made it sound. Doesn't she realize that I can't even keep my own head up over my own personal tidewater? I wondered. How does she expect me to be any good to anyone else?

But I learned. Part of it was seeing the old people's loneliness and part of it was needing to get away from myself. The nursing home was so different from my life with Guthrie. Where he'd given me sea breezes and the silence of early morning fog, there I was surrounded by the odor of disinfectants and old ladies who rocked dolls as if they were children.

I guess that's why I took so many walks at night; I had to get away from it all sometimes. Of course, many patients had relatives who came for visits or took them places, but it didn't stop the daily monotony. I tried to do what I could for them by picking bouquets of wildflowers for their rooms and telling the old folks about the bird's nest in the backyard oak tree, but I never felt it was enough.

Even when I started going to the public health clinic I had trouble talking about the baby. Of course seeing other infants gurgling and cooing, I felt a softening inside. But was that same miracle happening inside of me? That's what I couldn't put together. Fortunately the clinic doctor was very busy, so other than telling me to cut down on my sodium intake so my ankles wouldn't swell, he didn't have much to say to me. I don't know what I would've done if he'd started asking personal questions.

Mercifully, I was in my eighth month when Dr. Lahiri sat down across from me after my monthly examination. "Sienna, I think it's time we had a talk."

"Talk?" I felt a knot of fear form in my stomach, wondering if there was possibly something wrong with the baby.

"I've wanted to discuss your plans before this, but I was hoping you'd bring it up yourself. I know you're not married and that you're pretty much alone. What do you intend to do after the baby's born? Do you plan to keep it?"

Oh, God—just like that? It's not fair. What right does he have to dig so deeply? But it's not really his fault; after all, he doesn't know how mixed up everything is.

"I don't know."

"Why not?"

I glanced around, hoping for a way out, but there was none. The time for facing myself had come. "I—I'm afraid," I started slowly, watching my clenched fists grow white in my lap. "Doctor, I'm . . . illegitimate. My mother—she raised me by herself so I know it can be done. But I don't want my child growing up that way—not like I did, I mean. . . ." I had to take a deep breath before going on, letting out the dark secrets. "I was raised in a small, remote town because my mother couldn't afford to move away—or maybe she was afraid to take chances. Everyone knew about me and I guess back when I was born, people weren't so broadminded then. Or maybe it was the way my mother felt and acted; I don't know. But I think she hated me from the start."

"Why do you say that?"

I waited for the secret tears to subside, feeling the sharp pain of a belt on my back as if it were yesterday. "She . . . she used to beat me. A lot."

"Oh." He was looking at me so closely that I had to touch my smock to convince myself that I wasn't naked.

"I—I know today, they'd call it child abuse. All I know is my mother got mad many, many times. When she did she'd hit me—sometimes with a belt or strap, sometimes with her fists. She broke three of my ribs once and scalded me several times, but I never told the people at

55

the hospital what really happened. I was afraid to. You—you're the first person I've ever told."

"Even the baby's father doesn't know about your history?"

"N-no," I stammered. "I—I just wanted to forget."

"Sienna." The doctor touched my shoulder, rubbing a little of the tension away. "I'm sorry. That's so very hard for a child; it's natural to love a parent and traumatic to have that love thrown back at you. I'm sure you felt the community's disapproval during your childhood— and then to have your mother reject you in such a harsh way—you didn't think very much of yourself while you were growing up, did you?"

I stared at him, wondering, How does he know? How can he possibly understand so?

"You couldn't help but feel that way," he went on softly, making me listen to every word he said. "A child needs love as much as he or she needs air and nourishment, but you didn't get that. When a child feels deserted, that child doesn't believe in his or her own worth."

I felt the hot tears sting my cheeks and fought the impulse to bury my face in his chest. "I—I never could tell anyone how it was—how it really was, I mean. People—they always just said I was shy."

"I'm sure you were," he went on, gently rubbing my shaking shoulder. "I'm not a psychiatrist, but I'm guessing that when a certain young man came along offering you love, it seemed like the most wonderful thing that ever happened to you."

I nodded, thinking about Guthrie's eyes and how I'd lost myself in them, how I'd accepted his wandering life because it was better than no life at all.

The doctor smiled a little. "But it didn't last, did it?"

Miserable, I shook my head. "I couldn't . . . tie him down. I knew he'd think I got pregnant on purpose."

"And you were afraid he'd reject you the way your mother did. Sienna, you don't have any self-confidence, but the least you could have—and should have—done was tell him about the baby. It might've meant something to him, you know."

I shook my head vehemently, meeting the doctor's searching gaze for the first time. "No. He said he was experiencing life. He doesn't want mortgage payments and a regular job."

Dr. Lahiri's smile widened. "I used to think the same way myself, believe it or not. Maybe it's part of being young. But people change, Sienna. They meet someone who makes the nine-to-five life preferable to being alone."

That might be true for a lot of people, I thought sadly, but not for the footloose Guthrie I know. "It doesn't matter, anyway," I whispered, wiping my tears away. "He's gone."

The doctor straightened. "Yes. I guess that is in the past. What I'm concerned with now, though, is your future. Why did you say that you don't know whether or not you want to keep your child?"

Ten minutes ago I couldn't have told Dr. Lahiri, but he'd seen my tears now and knew things about me that no one else did. "I—I'm afraid of what—of what might . . . happen."

"Go on."

I looked up at his serious, kind, intelligent face, my eyes pleading with him desperately, searching his for answers. "What if I'm just like my mother, Doctor? I—I'm afraid I'll beat my child! I'm afraid it'll be the same story all over again!"

Dr. Lahiri rubbed his chin thoughtfully. "Sienna, I'm sorry. I can't help you resolve that. That's a job for a social worker." While he wrote some information down on a piece of paper, he told me about the state's social services agency and the men and women who were there to help people like me sort out their feelings. "Talk to them," he pressed. "If you decide to give up the baby they'll handle the adoption. And if you want to keep it, they can help you find childcare agencies or even get you some state aid for a while."

But by the time I'd had my first meeting with the woman from Social Services, I was so confused that I left her office in tears. There were so many things to think out, so many decisions to make. Do I want to sign my baby away? I agonized. Do I want to go on some short-term welfare right after I give birth? Or do I want to turn my infant over to strangers every day while I make a living for us? Difficult as those questions were, the one that overwhelmed me was facing what kind of mother I would be.

Dr. Lahiri was right; I didn't have much self-confidence. I was afraid of what might be living hidden inside of me—the sickness that would allow me to lash out at my innocent child. Oh, I knew I could love my child—that wasn't the issue. As it was, I already loved my baby desperately. But will I be any good as a mother? I wondered. My own mother couldn't have known what kind of parent she'd turn out to be. And I'm certainly not any wiser.

Then I woke up at three o'clock one morning with a knot in the small of my back. By ten that night I was the mother of a dark-haired baby boy with flecks of brown already in his eyes. Guthrie's eyes, I thought. He has Guthrie's eyes. Blessedly, exhaustion took over and I slept without dreams until the next morning, when a nurse brought my newborn son to me.

After she left I held him on my stomach, propping his head up against my raised knees so I could see his perfect face. He was so tiny, so helpless, his face so soft and trusting as he tried to focus on me. What is he thinking? I wondered. Does he sense the frightened pounding of my heart, the soul-deep doubts I carry inside of me? What right do I have to take responsibility for a new life? Me, with my mother's blood coursing through me. What kind of future can I give my infant? What if I'm just like my mother, filled with dark rages and an evil side known only to her innocent child? What if I'm a child-beater, too? Oh, God—better I never hold him again than subject him to that!

I guess my decision was made then. My son couldn't even hold up his head. What if I can't take his crying some night and I hurt him worse than I was hurt? I thought, my heart filling with terror. What if I kill him? Am I capable of that? I don't dare find out!

Later that day, the woman I'd been seeing from Social Services came by. "I stopped by the nursery," she said as she sat by my bed. "If I didn't have three of my own already I'd love one just like him!" She paused and looked at me searchingly, sobering. "So? What about it, Sienna? Have you made up your mind?"

I nodded. "I want to give him up for adoption."

"Oh." She was quiet a long time. "All right. It's your decision. I'll get the proceedings started as soon as possible."

"How long will it take?" All I wanted to do right then was run out of that hospital and keep on running for the rest of my life—as if it could be called a life.

"It depends. If it takes very long to contact the baby's father, it might be as much as six months."

Instantly, I felt the panic overwhelm me. "What are you talking about? My baby's illegitimate—I'm the only parent he has!"

"Not according to the law, Sienna," she gently explained. "In the wake of a 1972 Supreme Court decision, an unwed father has the same rights as the father of children born in a legal marriage. If he so desires, he is now entitled to a hearing on his fitness as a parent before his parental rights are terminated. Personally, I feel it's right and necessary for unwed fathers to be given the same considerations. After all, why shouldn't a man be allowed to raise his child if he wants to?"

"No! He doesn't even know about the baby! I don't even know where he is!" I started to sob.

"That's what I was afraid of." She shook her head. "Still, we're bound by law to try to contact him, Sienna. I'll place an ad in the area papers asking him to contact me, and if you know where he has family, you have to tell me, Sienna. If you'd told me you didn't know who the father is, I wouldn't have to do this, but even then, there would be even more delays and red tape and the court would have to inform the adoptive parents that it might not be a legal adoption. You can see how hard that would be for your son. Who knows when he might have a real home under such circumstances?"

"I see."

I didn't, though—not really. It was too much, having it all thrown at me all at once. As it was, I didn't want Guthrie to know—not ever. I figured he'd already forgotten about me—that he probably believed that I didn't love him anymore, if I ever did.

But what if they do find him? I wondered, my heart racing. Dear God, how could I ever face him?

In the end, though, I gave the social worker Guthrie's name and told her that as far as I knew, his parents lived in San Diego. He might be reached through them.

I went back to the nursing home empty-armed with a heart that had lost its reason for beating. No one said anything about the baby, but I could feel the questions in their eyes. No wonder, I thought. What kind of woman gives up her child and then goes on like nothing happened? Only, they couldn't see inside me and know my true agony.

As it was, I wanted to collect my small paycheck and jump on the first bus out of town, but I couldn't because I was still needed for the legal aspects of the adoption. Hard as it was on me, I did want to help my baby get out of foster care and into a real home as soon as possible; I knew I had to put his future ahead of my heartache. And even if Guthrie does hear about it, I decided, if he comes here, I'll convince him not to make things any harder for our son.

Yes, I was full of brave thoughts in the silence of my small room. But when the social worker called a week later and asked me to come to her office, my hidden terror bubbled to the surface. Guthrie was there.

"Sienna, I'm glad you could make it," Mrs. Wright said as she opened the door to the interviewing room and invited me in. "Look, I've got to make a phone call. Sit down and I'll be back as soon as I can."

I knew what she was doing the moment she closed the door behind her. Suddenly—deliberately—Guthrie and I were alone together. I dared to look at him and knew instantly that he knew what had happened and what I did. Then I couldn't look at him.

Guthrie stood and came to me, forcing me to face him. He still had a beard, but it was shorter and neatly trimmed. Gone were the ragged tennis shoes, the patched jeans, but he was still the same Guthrie . . . with his son's brown eyes. "Sienna, what is this about?" he asked, his voice ragged with restrained emotion.

"I . . . I didn't want it—not like this. I—I wasn't going to mix you up in this."

"I still don't know what you're talking about, Sienna." His brown eyes, the ones I used to read like a book, were closed to me. "All I

59

know is that my folks got a call saying that I have a son, and that I should come here and 'relinquish my parental rights' so he can be given up for adoption. What's going on, Sienna? Huh? Can you tell me at least that much?"

"It—it's true, Guthrie." Please, please, Guthrie—don't look at me like that. I'm falling apart. "That's why—why I left. I knew how you felt about—about being trapped. I didn't want you to think that I . . . got pregnant, on purpose."

"So you just decided not to tell me about the baby?"

"Yes." Why is it so hard for me to talk with him filling the room? How long will it take for this love to die?

"That doesn't make sense," he snapped, backing away. "Do you think I would've just let you wander off had I known? Jeez, Sienna—you didn't have anyplace to go and you didn't have a dime to your name! I've worried myself sick for months, wondering what happened to you!"

"Guthrie." I grabbed a chair for support, fighting the waves of emotion that tore through me. "You told me how it was with you. I accepted the ground rules—I accepted that you need to be free. That's why I couldn't stand the thought of you hating me because I got pregnant!"

"Good Lord!" He pounded his forehead. "Sienna, probably every guy in the world talks like that at some point in their lives! It doesn't mean that we can't change or that we really mean all that nonsense about never taking on any responsibilities! Why didn't you at least give me a chance? Couldn't you trust me enough?"

I sank into a chair and buried my head in my hands.

"You really are serious about this adoption, aren't you?" he asked after a long, silent, strained moment.

I had to look at him then. "Yes."

"Why?"

"I—I don't want the baby," I said shakily, even then thinking, No, Guthrie! No! It's not true! It's a lie! I do want our baby!

"You don't want—my God, Sienna. You're sick!" He whirled around and stared out the window. "My God, what did I ever see in you? And to think I . . . that I thought you needed someone—that you'd been alone too long—that you were just scared of something—something I didn't understand. But you . . . you must . . . like it that way." He turned back around to face me. "You accused me of being immature, but you're so selfish that it makes me sick."

I followed him with my bleeding heart as he slammed out the door. Then I felt the world crack away from me in great, big chunks.

It was done, over. The worst had happened. Guthrie, my love, knew about his son—and now he believed that his mother was a sick, selfish woman.

And I am, I thought. But not the way he thinks.

He didn't, couldn't know, I tried to tell my heart as I forced myself home. He'll never know the real reason. He doesn't even know that I'm illegitimate because I always wanted to be perfect for him. Uncomplicated. Not a problem in any way. Only, my lie had exploded around me and destroyed everything. But even though his words would echo in my heart for the rest of my life, I felt then that at least the worst was over.

Now our son will have a real home—a good, decent, stable, loving home, I thought, steeling myself with my resolve. That's what I have to cling to from now on—that one good thing. I can stand the pain as long as my son—our son—has a decent future ahead of him.

By the time I got back to the nursing home I'd made up my mind. Or rather, what was left of it. I decided I was going to leave at the end of that week—just as soon as I had enough money saved for a bus ticket out of state. From then on, I didn't know and I honestly didn't care. I kept thinking about Guthrie's anger, fearing he might return. I knew I couldn't bear that again. And even if I could somehow explain, I knew he wouldn't want to listen.

No, I thought as I began to pack my bag, in another state I'll be safe—from him, at least, if not from my own heartache.

Only I didn't have the chance to escape because the next morning the social worker called. Guthrie wanted his son.

"You can't mean it!" I sobbed. "But I signed him over to you!"

"Yes, but Guthrie has the same rights as you do, Sienna, remember? He's asking for custody of his child. I can't tell you how it'll turn out, but you deserve to know the whole story. His chances of getting his son are pretty good, I think."

"But why?" What can Guthrie possibly want with an infant? I wondered frantically. Does he actually think he can strap our newborn son on his back and head out for the highway?

"I don't suppose I'm telling you anything you shouldn't know," Mrs. Wright answered. "Guthrie's been living near his parents' and going to college, majoring in environmental biology. If he gets custody, his parents have agreed to take care of their grandson when he's in school or working. It's really no different from what any mother alone might choose to do."

It was too much! I'd thought that giving up my baby was more than I could ever bear, but to have Guthrie come back and turn everything upside down was inconceivable. It was all I could do to form the next question. "Did—did he say why, Mrs. Wright? I mean, I had no idea that he felt this way about children. He—he didn't before."

She sighed. "It's a pretty complicated situation, Sienna. Guthrie is a quiet young man, but this morning he told me that seeing his son

61

for the first time did things to him. Maybe fatherly instincts—maybe that's the right term for it. He said that just because you don't want the child doesn't mean that the baby has no parent to depend on."

He thinks I don't want our baby? How wrong Guthrie is! All of a sudden I couldn't go on, could barely breathe. Instead, I hung up on Mrs. Wright and collapsed to my knees, realizing, Guthrie thinks I'm some kind of heartless, loveless monster. After all, didn't he say as much to my face? But I couldn't just let things end like that because what if one day, he told our son what he believed about me?

No matter how it hurt, I realized I had to see Guthrie one more time and tell him the truth about my mother and me. Maybe, I thought, even if he can't ever forgive me, at least he'll understand and keep our child from despising me when he's old enough to know the truth.

My arms were almost too heavy for me to lift them when I knocked at the door of the motel room where Mrs. Wright had told me Guthrie was staying. Irrationally I hoped he wouldn't be there, and yet at the same time I was desperate to get everything over and done with before my courage failed me completely. Still, I drew back when Guthrie opened the door, afraid of the hardness in his eyes.

"I didn't expect this," he said, not asking me in. "I thought you were through with both our child and me."

"Please, Guthrie—don't talk like that," I begged. "I—there's something I have to explain to you."

"Of course. After all, explaining why you don't want your own child does take a little time, doesn't it?"

I grabbed the doorjamb and held onto it for support. "Please, Guthrie—don't hate me!"

"I don't," he said, his lips tight. "I simply can't understand you." Then he took my arm and pulled me inside, gently shutting the door behind me. "What's the matter? You look like you're going to pass out."

"No." Just the same, I stumbled toward a chair and sat without waiting for an invitation.

Guthrie sat in the chair opposite me, his eyes relentless on my face. "Well, then, why are you here? Don't tell me you object to me seeking custody of our son."

"That's not it." But it's part of it, I thought, believing that Guthrie was doing it simply to make up for what he believed I was. "I—I just want to explain things."

"Go on."

I started then, slowly and carefully telling him why I left that fateful morning without a word of good-bye.

After I'd said what I came to say, we were both silent. Guthrie looked thoughtful, and then finally he said, "You mean to tell me that you thought I'd hate you because you got pregnant? It takes two for that to happen, you know."

"But birth control was my responsibility. And you were always talking about girls who trap men that way. I—I couldn't bear to have you think the same of me." I took a deep breath and forged ahead. "Guthrie, I lived with you because I loved you. You offered me something I'd never felt before and I—I wasn't brave enough to stick around and watch it die—feel it die. It was easier for me to leave!"

He was still looking at me, and then he started shaking his head. "What about me, Sienna? Did you think that was the easiest way for me? One day I had a girl I loved sleeping beside me. The next day she was gone. That kind of kicked a hole in me, you know!" he cried heatedly.

"I'm sorry!" I moaned, leaning back. "I—I wasn't thinking clearly then." I shook my head miserably. "I guess I'm still not. At the time, though, I guess I thought you'd be upset for a while, but that you'd get over it. I figured at least I was leaving you with your freedom. That's what you always told me you needed most."

"Yeah. And I realize now that I didn't know what the heck I was talking about. Look, Sienna—back then, I was like every other idiot guy out on his own for the first time. I thought I had to make a big deal about how wonderful it all was to justify tramping around like some kind of aimless fool. After you left, though, I started to realize that it's a pretty empty way to live—at least, I think it is. That's why I went back to school when I couldn't find you; I finally realized that I have to have some kind of a goal."

"I'm glad," I said, wishing I could say the same thing about myself.

He shook his head dismissively. "Well, it's certainly not everything. But at least it's something." He looked down at his hands. "And then I saw our son," he whispered, his voice taking on an almost reverent quality. He shook his head. "I still don't understand it; I mean, he's just a baby. He doesn't even know who I am. But he fell asleep while I was holding him and telling him what a perfect little guy he is and I realized . . . he's mine." He looked up at me suddenly and I saw the tears shimmering in his dark eyes, so like our son's. "That's fantastic!" He sighed and closed his eyes briefly. "That—it—well, it just did things to me, Sienna. I looked at him and realized that I created him—or at least, half of him. It's a pretty amazing thought—one I'm still getting used to, I'll admit. But I have a son. Wow. It's like there's someone hanging onto me now. Someone who really needs me." He took a deep breath. "And I need him in a way I never knew I could need anyone."

"Oh," was all I could say. I was so choked up suddenly that I'm not even sure I got that much out.

"Sienna, it's none of my business," he said suddenly, coming to lean over me, "but why are you doing it this way? Why don't you want our child?"

Guthrie's face swam before me, lost in a flood of tears. "I'm afraid."

"Of what? Of raising him on your own? Of being a mother?"

I nodded. Indeed, that was it, in a way. But it was only part of the story, I knew—only the surface. I'd told the doctor and social worker about my childhood, but Guthrie was another story. We'd once shared so much that was good and I didn't want him to know anything about my dark, ugly past. But he was demanding—and deserving—the truth so I finally told him—I finally told him everything.

"You mean you were abused? My God, that's horrible!"

"Yes, but, it—it's over now. And I never meant for you to know," I managed. "I—I still don't want to talk about it—not any more, at least."

"But you have to, Sienna." He touched my shoulder gently, setting my aching flesh on fire. "You're making yourself sick holding all of that inside."

I looked at him plainly, letting him see the unshed tears brimming in my eyes. "Do you really think that talking about the time when my mother poured boiling water on me will change the past—that it will change anything that happened to me?"

"It wasn't your fault, Sienna. None of it was your fault. You have to understand that—accept it as truth."

"Wasn't it, though?" I'd never told anyone this part, but with Guthrie standing over me I lacked the strength to keep it in. "If I'd been good, she wouldn't have done those terrible, terrible things to me! She couldn't have—if she really loved me!"

"What? You mean to tell me that you actually think you deserved to be treated like that?"

"I don't know!" I cried. Suddenly, it was so hard for me to talk. "Every time I turned around she told me that I was bad—that I never should've been born!"

"No, Sienna!"

He took me in his arms then and I lacked the will to pull away. I was suffering and I dared to hope that maybe Guthrie's embrace could help make it all go away.

"No wonder you're afraid of becoming a mother! Just look at the example you had!"

"That's not it!" I said between sobs. "But I do wonder—what if I'm the same way? What if I'm incapable of motherly love? What if I'm only capable of hurting my baby?"

"And that's why you're giving him up?" He forced me to look into his eyes. "Because you think you're just like your mother?"

"I'm afraid to take the chance!" I cried. "I'm illegitimate, Guthrie—and I'd be raising my child the exact same way! But I won't hurt him! I won't!"

Guthrie and I stood there, our bodies not quite touching. My last cry seemed to hang in the room, not ending, covering the silence. After a long time, he lifted his head.

"Sienna, I want to say this right. It might take a while because I have to change the way I think about you. When you left I was worried, hurt, and angry, but I was getting over it. Then I heard about my son and what you planned to do. I wanted to shake you. But that was before I knew the truth."

"It . . . changes things?"

"Yes. You know, I used to think you liked being a mystery woman or something—like a gypsy out of that old Stevie Nicks song. I never dreamed that you were so messed up in your thinking, but I understand now. Anyway, what I'm trying to say is—I think we should give it another try."

"Another try?" A tomorrow with Guthrie in it? "Are—are you sure?"

"No, I'm not." He sighed. "But then, who knows anything for sure? All I know is that we have a son now. We'd be cheating him—cheating him terribly—if we didn't at least try to make a go of things, if only for his sake."

Guthrie and I went to San Diego with our son as soon as he was awarded custody of him. I know his parents didn't understand why we didn't get married right away, but Guthrie and I agreed that we weren't ready for any permanent, legally binding ties. We'd been apart for too long; one day at a time was all we could commit ourselves to at that juncture.

Kerouac, our tiny, precious son, held the answers I needed. While Guthrie worked and went to school, I learned how to be a mother. I learned about the exhaustion, the irritation that comes at two in the morning with a crying baby; I accepted that dirty diapers and messy bibs seemingly have no end.

More important, I discovered that Kerouac's tiny fist wrapped around my finger is like having everything good in the world within my grasp. His bright, happy smile and those beautiful, clear, brown eyes are all I will ever need. How could I have ever doubted my capacity to love my baby enough? Today, I am his prisoner—his willing, fulfilled, infinitely content prisoner.

"It's unbelievable," I told Guthrie one night recently as we watched Kerry trying to reach for the dangling stars in the mobile that hangs over his crib. "I had no idea that love can be so strong. It makes up for all the work."

Guthrie smiled. "It most certainly does. I'm telling you, Sienna—for an infant, this son of ours is mighty smart. A toothless grin and he has us right where he wants us—his adoring slaves for life! Speaking of which—are you ready to make an honest man out of me?"

"Yes," I answered. My heart echoed the word.

THE END

I JUST WANT TO
BE WITH YOU

When I saw the new girl at her locker, I took a deep breath and made my way over to her. There was something about her that made me want to make the extra effort.

"Hi. How are things going?" I asked. I stood near her and gave her my best smile.

She stared at me with her wonderful eyes and gave me a nervous smile. "It's okay."

My mouth went dry gazing at her angelic face that glowed with perspiration. My fingers ached to brush the hair out of her face.

"I'm glad you like it. By the way, my name is Jeremy Manning. You can count on me to answer any questions. There's no need for you to for you to feel like a stranger. Consider me your official welcome committee."

She stared at me with her wonderful eyes and gave me a nervous smile. "It's okay."

My mouth went dry gazing at Antonia's angelic face that glowed with perspiration. My fingers ached to brush the hair out of her face.

"I'm glad you like it. By the way, my name is Jeremy Manning. You can count on me to answer any questions. There's no need for you to for you to feel like a stranger. Consider me your official welcome committee."

"Gee, that's awfully nice of you, Jeremy. My name is Antonia Costas," she said, wiping her face with a tissue. Her hand trembled slightly. Still she smiled, revealing she had dimples. Then she shut her locker. "Nice talking to you, but I've got to run," she said as she hurried down the hall.

I felt hypnotized as I stood watching Antonia until she disappeared through the nearest exit. Noticing that she was sweating and the way her hand shook, I wondered if someone had said or done something to make her feel uncomfortable on the first day of school.

Suddenly, I was struck by a need to speak with her, to be near her. I had never felt that way before—about anyone.

I thought I heard someone calling me. It was Mercedes, my girlfriend.

Flinching at the sound of her voice, I froze in my steps and turned to face her.

"Jeremy, I've been waiting for you at your locker." Mercedes slipped her hand in mine, but she sounded exasperated. "Did you forget I told you to meet me here?"

I hadn't forgotten; I just hadn't cared much. I liked Mercedes a lot and she had been fun, but my feelings for her had changed a lot during the summer. And the change hadn't been good.

"Yeah, I had. I had to stop by to check with my guidance counselor about getting a schedule change," I lied. It was easier to do that than to get into an argument with her. She and I had been doing a lot of that lately. And it was mostly my fault.

"Let's go get something to eat. I refused to eat that mess they served for lunch in the cafeteria today." She tugged me toward the nearest door.

"I don't have the time, Mercedes. I have to go home and change my clothes and get ready for work. I have enough time to drop you home, though."

She looked disappointed. "What is it with you, lately? You're always full of excuses not to be with me."

I shrugged. "I have things to do. Come on, so I can drop you. I'm running late as it is." I released her hand and walked out the building and toward the parking lot to my car.

Once we were outside, I saw a group of kids in a circle. Several teachers rushed toward the area. I jogged in the direction to see what had happened. As I got closer, I saw Antonia sprawled on the parking lot.

The principal called for the nurse and paramedics on his walkie-talkie. Then the school security ordered us to step back.

Mercedes eased up beside me. "That's the new girl. What's the matter with her?"

"I don't know. It must be something serious or else they wouldn't have called the paramedics," I said. Filled with concern, I watched Antonia lying motionless.

When I heard the siren of the paramedic's van approaching, I listened to the speculation of the other students. There was talk of using drugs and about the Antonia being pregnant.

The nurse showed up and spoke to the medics as they carefully lifted Antonia on a gurney and placed her into the van. The nurse picked up Angela's things and climbed in with her.

I watched the van take off and hoped that Angela would be all right.

Walking away from the crowd, Mercedes was right on my heels. "Jeremy, wait up."

"Come on," I snapped.

"You don't have to be so grouchy. I'm not making you late. You were the one that had to be nosy," she said.

"I wasn't being nosy. I was only concerned. I met that new girl today and she seems nice,"

"So, are you trying to step to her?" she asked suspiciously.

"Mercedes, I'm not going to answer that. That girl was rushed to the hospital today. Be sensible."

Her face was pinched, and she looked as though she wanted to cry. "You've changed. I don't know you anymore."

I turned and looked at her. Yes, I had changed, but so had she. Mercedes and I used to have a lot of fun hanging out together. But the summer changed all that. Suddenly, she wanted to become more serious. I didn't know what I wanted. But she pushed to take our relationship to the next level, to sleep together. Even though I had some doubts, I went ahead anyway, and everything changed after that. I realized that I liked her a lot, but I hadn't loved her, and making love had made her more possessive. I guess, I should have expected that, but I hadn't.

And meeting Antonia made those feelings more apparent. I really did want to get to know her and to spend time with Antonia. I hadn't felt the same way about Mercedes. I just wanted to get away from her and out of her grip. But I didn't want to feel like a dog. After all, Mercedes and I had move love. But sex wasn't enough for me to stay with a man.

On the drive to Mercedes's house, I could feel her eyes burning into me. I was making her unhappy and she was making me feel guilty for not wanting her the way she wanted to be wanted by me.

Driving up in front of her house, I didn't turn off the ignition. "I'll give you a call later tonight," I said.

She looked sadly at me. "I want you to know that this past summer and what we shared was all about love for me."

"Mercedes, I care about you. What happened between us was special to me, too," I said in a comforting tone. It had been special, but not special enough. I wanted to end it with her, but I lacked the courage. I didn't want her to feel I had used her. "Let's not get into this now. We'll talk later."

Giving me a reluctant look, she opened the door of the car and walked away from me with her shoulders slumped.

I pulled away and tried not to be bothered by Mercedes's actions. I knew that I would have to tell her the way I felt soon because I kept thinking about Antonia. I didn't want to slip and say something about Antonia that would hurt Mercedes even more.

I was glad when I saw Antonia back in school a few days after her incident. Watching her from afar in the library, Antonia appeared to be the picture of health. She looked radiant. I sauntered over to her table and took a seat in front of her.

"Hi, Antonia," I said.

She looked up from her book. "Jeremy, right?"

"You remembered." I grinned, then leaned toward her. "It's good to see you back."

Antonia looked ill at ease.

"I was worried about you when I saw you passed out and—"

Without looking at me, Antonia's face colored, and she began to perspire. Then she rose, gathered her things, and left.

I stood with her and reached for her hand. "I'm sorry. You got sick."

Snatching her hand away, she cleared her throat. "You don't have to apologize. I just remember I have to be—be somewhere. I've—I've got a conference with one of my teachers." She hustled away from my table and out the library.

I dropped back down in my seat and heaved a frustrated sigh.

Mercedes appeared out of nowhere. She hovered over me, clutching a hall pass. "I saw you with that girl. Is there anything going on between the two of you?'

"Did you get out of class to spy on me?" I asked. I shifted my eyes from her and opened my history book to study. I felt guilty, but I didn't like what she was doing, the kind of girl she had become.

She took the seat next to mine. "I saw the way you were looking at her. I saw you take her hand. You're interested in more than a friendship? I recognize the look," she stated acidly.

I glared at her. "I hardly know her. I was only showing her my concern—"

"I'm going to show her some concern. I going to find her and let her know you've already got a girlfriend."

Frowning at her, I said, "No, I don't. Since that's how you're going to be, it's over."

A look of despair spread over her face. "You can't mean that," she whimpered.

"I do. I think it's best we go our separate ways," I said.

She settled back in her chair. It seemed as though she was deflated emotionally. "You've used me and now you want to lose me. I thought you'd be different, Jeremy. I never imagined you'd be one of those guys who'd only use a girl for one thing."

She bolted out of her seat. Her bottom lip quivered with a look that went from pain to anger. "I hate you, Jeremy!" she shouted. Then she stormed out of the library, knocking over a cart of books that were in her way.

She left everyone staring at me and making me feel like a monster as my schoolmates murmured over the breakup scene they'd witnessed. I slumped in my seat and pretended to read again. I was embarrassed and knew everyone had seen what happened—and those who hadn't seen it, would hear about it soon enough. I glanced at the big library clock and noticed that it was ten o'clock. The only thing that gave me comfort at the moment was that my day couldn't get any worst than it had.

By the time my lunch bell rolled around, I decided not to eat in the cafeteria. I didn't want to run into Mercedes or any of her girlfriends whom I knew would attack me verbally for breaking up with Mercedes.

Instead, I headed outside to sit on the bleachers on the football field, so that I could be alone to think. As I climbed midway, I was surprised to see Antonia, sitting by herself and eating from her lunch bag. She looked as lonely as I felt. But she was a sight for sore eyes. Her hair tossed in the gentle breeze and when she turned her head slightly in my direction, I admired her profile and her delicate features. Once she was done eating, she pulled out her disc player and placed headsets on her ears. She leaned back and closed her eyes as though she had slipped away from her environment.

I had eaten only part of my lunch when I decided to make another effort to befriend Antonia. I descended the bleachers and walked over to her. When I touched her on the shoulder, she lurched forward, then turned and scowled.

She removed her headset and said, "You frightened me, slipping up on me that way."

I dropped down beside her. "I didn't mean to. I only wanted to apologize for this morning."

She sighed and offered me a hint of a smile. "There's nothing for you to apologize for. I overreacted. I suppose, I'm still embarrassed by what happened to me the other day. It was kind of you to ask about me."

I felt relieved that she had taken on a new attitude toward me. "Eating out here is better than in that noisy cafeteria. It's a great day, huh?"

"Yeah, it is. Being this is my first day in school since that day, I was a bit anxious about going into the lunchroom," she said.

"You shouldn't feel bad about getting sick," I said.

She smiled sadly. "It's just awkward for me being new and not knowing anyone."

"You don't have to feel that way. You know me, and I'm more than willing to be your friend," I said.

She stared at me with a twinkle in her eyes. "How can I refuse kindness or your friendship?"

The first bell sounded for the beginning of class.

Antonia stood. "Well, we'd better head back into the building. I have a class on the third floor."

I jumped to my feet. "So, do I. Let me walk you to class."

"I'd like the company," she said, smiling.

My spirits lifted. I'd like feeling as though I had gained her confidence.

During the next few weeks, Antonia and I spent a lot of time together at school. I awoke each morning with Antonia on my mind. I was becoming hooked on the sound of her voice, her smile and that wonderful look in her eyes whenever we talked. Though I had managed to get her to think of me as a friend, I wanted to take her out and to have her see me as more than that. She seemed to like me, but there was a wall I couldn't get beyond.

For some reason or another, Antonia never invited me to her house. Whenever I suggested she and I take in a movie or attend a football game, she'd come up with an excuse why she couldn't go. Sometimes, she'd interrupt our conversation abruptly and rush away like she had something urgent to attend to. I didn't question her because I didn't want to lose the bit of trust I had built with her.

But there was certainly something going on, I didn't know if she had a boyfriend or if the one of the other rumors were true, but I was determined to find out. Antonia had a secret.

One day while I had gotten Antonia to share a pizza with me after school at a nearby restaurant, she told me her eighteenth birthday was that Friday. I insisted she let me take her to the football game and the dance that followed in the gym. Much to my surprise, she agreed.

I decided that her birthday would be the best time for me to admit the secret attraction. I even planned to buy her a gift that I'd hoped would encourage her to think of me as more than "just a friend." I assumed she didn't have a boyfriend because she was spending the day with me. Or was she trying to make someone jealous. I couldn't think about that. I just had to think about letting her know my true feelings and hoping her were moving in the same way.

I had volunteered to pick up Antonia to bring her to the game, but she insisted on meeting me there. She had some errands to run with her mother. Later, her mother would drop her at the game, she explained.

At the end of the first quarter of our high school football game, I was beginning to fear that Antonia was going to stand me up. While I stood near the concession stand where we'd agreed to meet, Mercedes confronted me.

"Jeremy, why aren't you up in the bleachers cheering?" she asked.

"Hi Mercedes," I said coolly. "I'm waiting for a friend." I focused my attention on the field to keep from meeting her intense stare.

"Could that friend be Antonia? It looks to me like you two are becoming quite an item. You couldn't wait to dump me to get her," she said. "What do you see in her? Everyone says she's strange. You're the only person she talks to, but I guess you want it that way."

"What does that mean?"

"You only want a girl who doesn't have a brain and won't ask you for anything. How can she ask you for anything when she can't give you what you want? Oh, I forget. She can give you what you want all the time. You can't get pregnant if you're already pregnant."

"What are you talking about?" I asked angrily.

"Well, she's either pregnant or an addict or both. She's already been seen in the bathroom with her drug stuff. I know you like playing the hero, so now you can really play it to the max."

"I don't know where you got that idea."

"I know that's why you broke up with me. I wasn't needy enough for you. Well, I played as needy as I could. Now, I'm back to being myself. So, you and your girl can do whatever you want." Then she rolled her eyes and walked away.

Is Antonia pregnant? Is that why she's always acting so strange? She doesn't have to tell me, but I thought she trusted me. I thought we were at least, friends. And what did she mean about drug stuff. I know Antonia is not using. At least, I don't think she's an addict.

I was starting to feel angry and used. Had Antonia been using me? Was I supposed to be a substitute dad for her baby? Or was she abusing drugs. That would explain the perspiration and nervousness. I just couldn't believe it. Antonia didn't seem like that type of girl.

I remained standing at the concession stand. Antonia walked toward me looking as pretty as ever. She smiled as she approached me.

"I'm sorry that I'm late but I—I wasn't feeling too good. I started not to come, but I thought of how much you wanted to help me celebrate my birthday," she said.

I pushed Mercedes's cruel words out of my mind. I reached for Antonia's hand to lead her to the bleachers. "You're here now. Let's have some fun."

And we did. Antonia seemed very relaxed. When we left the game to attend the dance, Antonia was raring to go. She wanted to dance to every song. I had bought her a present and had planned on giving it to her at the end of the dance. Along with the gift I was intended on laying my emotions on the line too.

While Antonia and I laughed, talked and danced, I could feel Mercedes and her crew of girlfriends scrutinizing us. In order to give them something really to talk about, I kissed Antonia on the lips.

Antonia's eyes widened with surprise. Then a smile lifted the corners of her mouth.

"What was that all about?"

I returned her smile. "To wish you a happy birthday and to let you know I have feelings stronger than friendship for you."

Her eyes sparkled. "I—I don't know what to say."

"Antonia, I've been crazy about you from the moment I first saw you at school. I've heard of love at first sight, but I thought it was all a bunch of junk until I saw you." I held her to me and hugged her. "Give me a chance to be more than your friend."

Suddenly, I felt her going limp. She pushed me away and teetered on her feet. Then she collapsed on the floor.

I dropped to my knees and lifted her shoulders and called out her name.

A couple of teachers who were chaperones appeared and a crowd gathered around us. One of the teachers made me step aside.

Feeling helpless, I stood watching while they made everyone back away. Soon, the paramedics arrived at the dance and took Antonia away to the hospital again.

Determined to be with her, I rushed from the gym and toward the parking lot. I halted when I heard Mercedes calling me, urging me to wait.

"I don't have time for you. I've got to go check on Antonia," I said, fumbling with the lock on my car door.

"I told you, didn't I? What will it take for you to see she's not the girl for you?" Mercedes said in a spiteful tone.

"You don't know anything about Antonia. You're just jealous." I said, opening my door and climbing in my car.

As I started my car, Mercedes tapped on my window. "Shame on you. How can you want a druggie?"

I gave her a scorching look and zoomed off the parking lot.

On the drive to the hospital, I considered Mercedes's words. I thought of how mysterious Antonia was. I remembered how she would get listless and her hands would tremble. Sometimes, we'd be outside in the brisk fall air and she would break out in a sweat. Is Antonia into drugs? I wondered briefly. Then I felt ashamed of my thoughts. It just couldn't be. There had to be something else going on.

This was the second time she had passed out and had to be rushed to the hospital. What was it that she was hiding from me? I mused, pulling onto the hospital emergency room entrance.

Entering the hospital, I went to the reception desk and immediately asked about Antonia. The clerk told me she had just been brought in, and I would have to wait. A few moments later, I overheard a couple ask for Antonia Costas. They were escorted to the examining rooms.

Later, I saw the man exit, and I approached him, "Mr. Costas?"

He studied me. "Yes."

"Uh—I'm a friend of Antonia's. My name is Jeremy. She and I were at a dance when she collapsed. Is she going to be all right?"

"She's going to be fine. She only had a reaction to her new medication."

"Excuse me. I don't understand," I said.

"Antonia is diabetic. She's been dealing with this since she was four years old."

I was shocked. I only knew of older people who suffered from diabetes, not anyone my age.

"She must not have been eating right. You say, you were at a dance with her? Did she do a lot of dancing?" Antonia's father asked.

"Well, she and I did. We were having a good time. Today's her birthday."

"I know. She's eighteen today. That must be the reason her blood sugar dropped and caused her to pass out. She has to eat more whenever she's active. But knowing my Antonia, she probably figured she would be okay until she got home. She's always saying that the diabetes makes her feel like a freak. She hates having to check her blood sugar three or four times a day. She hates having to run to nurse's office. She doesn't want anyone to know."

I stood, listening to Mr. Costas and feeling sorry for Antonia. And that was probably the reason she kept to herself. That way, she didn't have to let anyone know.

"The doctor's have given Antonia something to stabilize her. They want to give her some time to see how she does before sending her home," Mr. Costas explained. "I'd better go in and check on her." He looked up toward the sky before continuing. "It's mighty kind of you to come and hang around to check on her."

"Uh—I was concerned. Do you mind if I see her?" I asked.

He stared at me and smiled. "Come on. I suppose it'll be okay. I'll tell the doctor you're her boyfriend." He chuckled.

I followed him into emergency and back to the exam room where Antonia was with her mother. Mr. Costas introduced me to his wife. Antonia sat on the side her bed and wouldn't look at me."

"Antonia, you never mentioned that you had made such a good friend. We appreciate your interest," Mrs. Costas said as she turned toward me. "Antonia doesn't usually make friends. She stays to herself too much for me. I'm glad to see that's ending."

"Mom!" Antonia exclaimed.

"Well, it's the truth dear." Mrs. Costas grinned and patted her daughter on the knee. Then she grabbed her husband by the arm. "Let's go finish the paperwork. The doctor says she should be fine and can go home."

Left alone, I sat beside Antonia and took her by the hand. "You scared me. I thought maybe I had made you sick." I laughed softly. "Your father told me you're diabetic."

She lifted her eyes to meet mine. "This is so embarrassing. I was having too much fun even to consider what would happen if I hadn't eaten a snack or had some juice to keep from blanking out." She grew silent. "Everyone is still whispering about the last incident I had on the first day of school. People think I'm either pregnant or an addict. I hate this. I'm sick of everything I have to do all the time. It's all such a pain." She looked as though she wanted to cry.

I placed my arm around her shoulder and pulled her to me. "Don't stress. You'll going to be all right as long as you take your medicine," I said, wondering if this was really so. "Besides, I'm going to be around to keep tabs on you."

She sighed and gazed at me. "What a way to end my birthday?"

Suddenly, I remembered the gift I had bought for her. I fumbled in the pocket of my jacket and pulled out the neatly wrapped small box and handed it to her. "Happy birthday, Antonia."

As she accepted it, her expression was full of awe. "Jeremy, you're so sweet. Thanks." She began ripping away the paper to reveal a golden jewelry box. "This is the first gift I've ever gotten from a guy." She lifted the lid and gasped at the gold necklace with the butterfly pendant. "This is so cute." She gave me an appreciative hug.

"The lady told me the butterfly is a symbol of hope. It suited my feelings for you."

Her action pleased me. I returned her embrace, loving the feel of her in my arms. I released her. "Due to unfortunate situations, you didn't get a chance to answer my question. Do you remember what I said?" I brushed her hair with my hair while staring into her eyes.

"You wanted to be more than friends with me," she said quietly.

"Well, how do you feel about it?" I waited for her answer with anticipation.

Antonia lifted the necklace out of the box and held it up, admiring the butterfly. She met my gaze. "Would you fasten this around my neck? Whenever I look at it or touch it, I'll be comforted knowing I'm a lucky girl to have such a great guy to care for me in spite of everything."

Once I had fastened the necklace around her neck, I kissed her on the cheek. She made me the happiest I'd ever been. I couldn't think of a better way to complete our last year of high school. I knew the memories we'd share as a couple would last in our hearts forever. Whenever we were together, people would stare and smile. It was obvious that the love that had blossomed between was better than anything that money could buy.

THE END

76

I WAS BEAT UP
AT THE PROM

The only empty seat on the bus was next to me. And, of course, Ray had to sit in it. It wasn't enough that he had humiliated me at the lake; he had to sit next to me, too. I had hoped he'd be too embarrassed and would move to the back. Unfortunately, my pain didn't bother him enough. He sat right next to me. I turned my head to look at the window. Maybe he'd realize that I didn't want him in my universe.

"Hi, Jasmine," he said softly.

My mouth was dry. "Hello, Ray," I mumbled.

He was fiddling with a charm that dangled from his jacket zipper. I gave him that charm the same day he gave me his class ring. But I didn't have his ring anymore.

I felt awful, thinking about it, having Ray near me again.

"Look, Jasmine," he said, "no hard feelings, huh? We're—we're still friends, aren't we?"

As if I could ever forgive him!

"Why do you care if we're friends or not?" I said. "I hear that you're not exactly lonely these days."

He gave me a funny look, as if I shouldn't mention that, even though it was all over school about him and Jenny Hoag.

Finally, he said: "I suppose you've heard plenty. It's all true, too."

He was practically bragging about it! The girls with the worst reputations in school were in Jenny Hoag's group, and Jenny was the worst. I didn't see anything for Ray to brag about—at least not to me.

I rang for my stop and got up. Ray moved his legs so I could get out.

"Listen, Jasmine, could I walk you home?" he asked. "I just want to talk to you?"

He put his hand on my arm, but I jerked away. "No, thanks," I said, and I left as fast as I could. I was shaking, and I was so angry. And at the same time, I felt like I would burst out crying any minute. . . .

It was only two weeks before that we'd gone on the picnic at the lake. Paulette Stewart made all the plans, and, like always, I felt wonderful being with Ray.

But that day, for the first time, a couple of the boys in our crowd brought bottles and passed them around. Ray was in on the drinking, but I didn't realize what it was doing to him. When he asked me to walk up the shore with him, I never thought to say "no." I even felt a trembling feeling of excitement, knowing that he'd want to kiss me when we were alone.

But almost as soon as we got out of sight of the rest of the crowd, Ray acted different. He kissed me different. It scared me at first, because it made me feel so strange.

I tried to joke. "Take it easy!" I said.

He didn't let me go. "I'm tired of taking it easy," he whispered, holding me tight. Then, suddenly, his hands were all over me. He'd never touched me like that before.

"Ray, stop it!" I gasped. I jerked away, and my blouse came all unbuttoned. "Ray! Stop!" I said. "I mean it!"

He smiled then, a scary smile. His eyes were half closed. "I thought you loved me, honey," he muttered.

I tried to get out of his arms, but he was holding me too tight. "I do love you," I said, "but I don't like it when you act like this!"

"If you love me, then you ought to prove it!" he insisted.

All at once, I was afraid of him. He'd never been so demanding before, and he was awfully strong. I turned my face away.

"I want to go home, Ray," I said. "Right now!"

He started pulling at me again. "Not yet," he said. "Later—after you show me how much you love me."

I was fighting hard to get away from him. "Ray Abato, you're drunk!" I told him, and I started to sob. "Now get your hands off me and take me home!"

I hit out at him, but he just laughed. It was awful. My clothes were all twisted, and he kept touching and grabbing me. I wanted to scream, but I would have died if any of the others came and saw us. Panicky with terror, I jerked one arm free and slapped Ray across the face as hard as I could.

It shocked us both. I sat there shaking and sick and scared. Ray's mouth hung open, and then he slowly rubbed his cheek. The look in his eyes was terrible.

I started to get up, but he grabbed my wrist and held me tight. "If you won't do it, I'll find somebody who will," he said.

"Go ahead!" I sobbed. "I don't ever want to see you again!"

I yanked the chain from my neck that held his ring. I took it off the necklace and threw it at him. Then I ran down the path along the shore, away from the picnic area. There was a drive-in nearby, and I raced toward it.

When I got there, I went to the phone booth and called a cab. I huddled miserably in the booth until it came. . . .

All the despair and horror came back after I saw Ray on the bus. Maybe it wouldn't have hurt me so much if I hadn't liked Ray so much—and trusted him. But that's what made it worse.

I was washing the supper dishes that night when Mom rolled her wheelchair to the kitchen door. "Jasmine," she said, her face glowing with excitement, "I've got something to show you."

Then she looked at me more closely, and her smile faded. "Honey, you're crying!" she said.

I shook my head. "I—I just got soap in my eye," I lied. I rubbed my eyes hard so she'd believe me.

No matter how hard it was, I wasn't going to tell Mom about what had happened. She liked Ray, and she was so happy for me and for all the fun I was having in school. I just couldn't tell her it was all over. I didn't want her worrying and feeling miserable about me. She'd certainly had enough trouble as it was.

I was seven when my father died. Mom got really sick the same year. Lots of women would have just cracked, I guess, facing all that tragedy. But not Mom. I never heard her complain.

Daddy's insurance went quickly, paying for her medical expenses. But Mom had plans for a dressmaking business, and just as soon as she could, she got started in it.

At first, I think women came to her because they felt sorry for her. But Mom wasn't having anyone's sympathy. She did work that was just beautiful, and before very long, she had more work than she could handle. The wonderful thing was that you never noticed that she was disabled. Instead, you noticed how good she was and how enthusiastic she was about her work. I guess she was the most wonderful mother anybody ever had.

I dried my hands on my apron and followed her into her sewing room. Then I saw the dress in the middle of the room. It was a strapless white formal. The skirt was slimming and tight. It looked very chic, very retro.

"Oh, Mom," I said, "it's just beautiful! It's the most beautiful dress you've ever made!" I couldn't keep from going over and touching it. "Who's it for?"

"You!" Mom said. "It's your prom dress, Jasmine. I wanted it to be a surprise."

Prom! I'd forgotten all about it! It was only two weeks away. Ray was supposed to be my date—and, of course, that was off now. But the surprise and hurt in Mom's eyes at my expression made me bite back my tears. I bent over and kissed her. Somehow, I managed to thank her. I couldn't bring myself to tell her that I wouldn't be wearing it.

I kept on putting off telling her. The dress hung in my closet, and I hadn't even tried it on. At first, I thought maybe I'd get another date. But I didn't. Most of my classmates were already paired off for the prom. Even if they weren't, I'd found out fast enough that when you'd been out of circulation as long as I had, the boys just stayed away.

I finally broke down and told my girlfriend, Maggie Tilton, about it. Of course, I didn't say what had happened between Ray and me.

"Maybe Ray plans to keep the date," she said. "I mean after all it is our prom."

"Well, even if he does plan to, I don't," I told her. "After the stories I've been hearing about him and Jenny Hoag, I wouldn't want to go."

"Isn't it awful?" she gasped. "The way Jenny hangs onto him, it's just sickening! Even Ray looks embarrassed! She must think she owns him. I heard she even picked a fight with some girl because she thought she was playing up to Ray."

I felt sick, hearing it. "Honest, Maggie, I'm not interested," I said.

Maggie took the hint. "Well, I'll spread it around that you haven't got a prom date," she said. "But frankly, Jasmine, it's pretty late. The tickets aren't even on sale anymore. But I'll try."

"Okay," I said. "Only, Maggie, don't make it obvious—like I'm begging for a date. I don't want Ray to think—"

Maggie smiled. "Trust me," she said.

I kept telling myself I'd get a date somehow. Whom it was with didn't matter. All that mattered was for Mom to have the joy of seeing me in the dress she'd made. That, and showing Ray that a girl didn't have to act like Jenny Hoag to get dates.

But days went by, and I still didn't get a date. I decided I'd have to tell Mom. I felt terrible, thinking how heartbroken she'd be. I had a speech all rehearsed, and I was going to tell her at dinner Tuesday night.

But before I had a chance, she said something that stopped me. "Only a few more days till the prom, Jasmine!" she burst out. "I'm so excited—really, I feel like I'm going! I never had the chance when I was in high school, but this makes up for it!"

She kept on talking that way, and my heart sank.

"Will you try on your dress for me tonight?" she begged.

I tried to tell her about not going, but I couldn't. Besides, there was still time. Maybe I'd have a date, yet. . .

When I saw Maggie in school the next day, I asked right off: "Any luck?" She just shook her head.

I guess she tried to be subtle about asking around, but she didn't fool anyone. By lunchtime, the kids started talking. A couple of them even made wisecracks right to my face. I wanted to die. I was so embarrassed.

And then when I was at my locker after school that day, Jenny Hoag came up to me. "Hi, Jasmine," she said, a nasty grin on her face. "I want to return this piece of junk." She held out her hand, and in it was the heart I'd given Ray. "Take it!" she said. "It belongs to you. When a guy's mine, I don't like him wearing some other girl's label."

I took the charm and turned away, hoping she'd leave me alone. I felt like I was going to cry.

She grabbed my shoulder. "I hope you heard me right, Jasmine," she snapped. "I said Ray's mine! Don't you forget it! I've been hearing all the sob stories. You know the ones you've been spreading around about not having a prom date. Well, if you're hoping Ray will come running back, you're crazy."

I jerked my shoulder to get her hand off me. "I don't want him," I said. "You're welcome to him."

"Okay," she said. "Just so we understand each other. Because if you louse things up for me, I'll make you so sorry you'll wish you'd never been born."

I walked home alone that day. I went past the place where Ray and I used to hang out. Then I heard some voices yelling. They asked me how much would I pay them to take me to the prom. Then they all roared with laughter. I wished I could die on the spot.

I rushed home as fast as I could. I sneaked up to my room and closed the door, sobbing so hard I was afraid Mom would hear. Then I saw my prom dress hanging on my closet door, and, for a minute, I just hated it.

When I was able to stop crying, I washed my face and went downstairs. Mom was in the kitchen, getting dinner, and I could tell from the way she kept looking at me that she was just bursting with some big news.

I finally got it out of her. "Ray called this afternoon," she said, "to find out what kind of flowers to send you for the prom."

I froze. "Ray?" I gasped.

"Well, who else would it be?" Mom said. "He asked if he could come over tonight, too." She smiled at me. "I didn't think you'd be too busy. I told him to come."

I sat there, numb with shock. I didn't want to see Ray. Not that evening or ever. Sure, I wanted a prom date—but not with him! Maybe he thought I wanted one so badly, I'd do anything to get it.

He came at seven-thirty. I hurried to the door to let him in so I could talk to him without Mom hearing.

"Of all the sneaky tricks!" I whispered. "Getting Mom to invite you here! I said I didn't want to see you again, Ray, and I meant it!"

His lips pressed together, tight and mad. "I want to talk to you," he said. "And we still have our prom date, remember?"

I shook my head. "No, we don't! Not after what you did—"

"Are you two going to stay in the hall all evening?" Mom called.

Then we had to go inside. Oh, I'll admit I sort of liked it, having Ray there again. I was used to him, after going steady so long. And I still hadn't got over that thrilled feeling whenever he was close to me. But all I had to do was remember the way he treated me the last time, and I'd start hating him again. He treated me as though my thoughts didn't matter. He acted as though I was a cheap tramp.

We had cookies and sodas and watched music videos. We didn't say much. Mom was in the next room, but the door was closed.

"How come it's all over school that you're desperate for a prom date?" Ray asked. "I asked you months ago."

I was so tense and jumpy I almost bit his head off. "What do I have to do, Ray—spell it out for you? I'm not going out with you. I want to be able to respect myself—even if you don't."

Ray didn't look at me. He stared down at his hands and he kept biting his lip. "I'm sorry, Jasmine," he told me. "I was drunk, but I guess that's no excuse. All I want is—is for things to be like they were before. I—I still feel the same about you. Please—at least go to the prom with me. I give you my word. I won't ever get rough with you again. I was crazy that night."

I wanted to believe him. I still liked him. I couldn't help that. But all I had to do was remember that he was running around with Jenny Hoag, and I couldn't believe him. Boys went with her for only one reason.

"Jenny gave me back the heart charm," I said. "The one I gave you."

Ray's head snapped up. His eyes were wide and mad. "I thought I lost it!" he said. "She took it! I swear I didn't give it to her, Jasmine! No matter what you think of me, I'm not that low!"

"What's the difference?" I said. "Jenny's your girl now. Take her to the prom. You'd probably have more fun with her. Don't worry about me."

Ray put his hands over his face. His voice was muffled. "Jasmine, how long do you want me to go on begging? Sure, I was mad after that day. But it was me I was mad at, not you! I picked up Jenny that night, and—well, she's been hanging onto me ever since. But she doesn't mean anything to me. You know she couldn't. She's anybody's girl—any time. And no matter how it looks, there's nothing between us—nothing like you think. Just give me another chance. That's all I ask!"

I didn't know if I'd ever feel I could trust him again. But maybe he was sorry—maybe I owed him another chance.

"Okay, Ray," I said. "I'll go with you. Maybe I'm crazy, but I will."

Things were nicer after that, almost like before. Just when he was leaving, he asked if he could have the heart charm back. I gave it to him. "I'd like to give you back my ring too, Jasmine," he said. "But I'll wait. I'll wait until you know that things are right between us."

He didn't try to kiss me. He just held my hand for a minute. "For the first time in weeks, I feel like a human being again!" he said.

I felt better, too. The next day at school was easier because I didn't have to worry about not having a prom date. I told Maggie what happened.

"See? I knew everything would work out!" she said.

When I was walking home, I was actually happy—even humming to myself. I took a short cut that went down along the lake. I didn't know then that I was being followed.

I was walking past an empty lot when I heard steps behind me. Then I heard some girls talking and laughing. All of a sudden, one of them said something loud enough for me to hear.

"Maybe you'd better warn her better, Jenny," she said. They all started laughing again, and I felt myself go cold and start to shake all over.

I heard them start to run up behind me, and I tried to get away. But there were five of them, and they made a circle around me. I couldn't run. I couldn't get away. They were tough, and the words they used were just filthy. They kept reaching out at me, pinching me, yanking my hair, and grabbing my knapsack. They were so quick and mean; I didn't have a chance.

Then Jenny came and stood in front of me, so close I couldn't move a step. "Ray's wearing that crazy charm again!" she yelled. "How come? I thought I warned you good."

I was so panicky I couldn't answer. Two of the girls grabbed my arms and twisted them behind me.

"I guess you still figure Ray's taking you to the prom," Jenny went on. "Well, that's where you're wrong. He's mine, and I'm not letting a nothing like you cut in on my time."

"We had a date for the prom before he ever met you," I choked out.

Jenny's hand shot out and slapped me hard across the face. "That date's off—as of now!" she said. Then she grabbed my hat and yanked it off my head. "Maybe we ought to fix it so you won't be able to go to any prom—ever!"

I struggled to break away from them, but they closed in around me. I couldn't get free. They kept on tormenting me—pinching me and pulling my hair and shoving back and forth till I was dizzy and scared. I thought I was going to faint.

And then all of a sudden, just as fast as they came, they all disappeared. "Think it over, Jasmine," Jenny said. Then they left.

I didn't stop shaking all the way home. I was very grateful that it was the day Mrs. Bolton, our neighbor, drove Mom in for her regular doctor's appointment. If she'd seen me, I don't know how I could have explained my appearance. I had a horrible throbbing headache, but I took a couple of aspirins and didn't mention anything about it to Mom when she got back.

Ray called at eight. I couldn't tell him what happened, either. Mom was in the same room.

But I did the next day at school. I told him everything. I was crying by the time I finished. "You talk to her, Ray!" I said. "Otherwise she'll never leave me alone! Ray, I'm scared of her!"

His face was white. "Okay. I'll—I'll talk to her, Jasmine," he said.

Ray promised to walk me home that night. I was too scared to go alone, even as far as the bus stop. I asked him if he'd tasked to Jenny, and he said

"Yeah, I tried. But she didn't go for it much. Don't worry about her, though, Jasmine. What can she do?"

Well, I wasn't just worried. I was scared. "I wish the prom was over!" I said. "That'll be the end of this mess."

Ray nodded. "I'm sorry, honey," he said. "But I'll never do anything to hurt you again—I swear it!"

Well, all that sounded fine and noble but it didn't make me feel any less scared. By the time the night of the prom came, I was a nervous wreck.

The flowers Ray sent were tiny pink roses to wear in my hair. The dress fit perfectly. I felt beautiful in it. When I came out, Mom's eyes filled with tears. It made me shiver inside. I was so glad. For a minute, it was worth it, all I'd gone through. Just seeing her happiness made it bearable.

There was a party at Yasmine Tolliver's before the dance. I felt myself start to tighten up when I saw the liquor being passed around. Half the guys were on their way to getting drunk. I turned ice cold with worry about Ray.

But when Own Frame came up to us and started to pour some whiskey into Ray's glass of punch, Ray stopped him.

"Not for me," he said.

Owen laughed and started kidding him. "Everybody's doing it," he said. "What's the matter with you?"

Ray just smiled at him. "Not tonight. I don't want to drink and drive," he said. "I'm on the wagon."

Owen shrugged and went away, and Ray smiled down at me. I guess it finally sank into my thick head then that he'd really meant what he said about being sorry and swearing it would never happen again. Suddenly, I was so happy! I wasn't worried or scared anymore, and I put my arm through Ray's and smiled up at him.

We left for the dance soon after. I was so excited I could hardly wait. Ray and I danced practically every dance together. I was having a great time.

After awhile, lots of my classmates went out and sat in their cars to sneak drinks. But Ray and I went out behind the gym and sat on the hill overlooking the lake. There were other couples there, too, but we found a place off alone and Ray spread his jacket on the ground for me to sit on. We watched the night boats on the lake, their lights tiny and winking, and we didn't even talk. Ray had his arm around me, and we just sat close together. I'd never felt so happy in my life.

When someone came up behind us, Ray turned around. All of a sudden, his arm tightened around me. Then I heard him catch his breath.

Before I could even turn, I heard Jenny Hoag's voice. "Well, here they both are!" she hissed. She'd been drinking. I could smell it, even though she was standing a couple of yards away from us. She was wearing jeans and a jacket. Her face looked mean and mad in the dim light.

Ray got up. "Come on, Jasmine. We'd better get back inside," he said, his voice tense and nervous. He grabbed me and tried to hurry me past her. My legs were shaking and my mouth had gone dry.

For a minute, I thought she wasn't going to cause any trouble. She didn't make a move until we'd walked right past her. Then, suddenly, she made a grab for me.

Ray let out a yell. He tried to push me behind him, but Jenny had my arm and wouldn't let go. Her fingers squeezed tight. I fought to get away from her, but I couldn't. I was sobbing and begging Ray to help me.

The band had returned from their break and everyone had gone back inside. There was no one but us. Even if there had been, they'd never have heard Ray's yell or my strangled screams over the blare of the band.

Ray was trying to pull Jenny's hands off me. I saw his face, the way his teeth were clenched. And I felt him pulling and jerking at Jenny. Then all of a sudden, he let go. His face had a surprised look on it, and then he slowly slid to the ground. Behind him, I saw Gayle Loring grinning and sneering at me.

"That'll take care of your boyfriend for a while!" she said, holding up her hand. She showed how she'd snapped it against the back of Ray's neck to knock him out.

I was fighting wildly, kicking and struggling to break Jenny's hold on me. But she was much stronger than I was. I tried to claw at her, hit her, bite her hands, anything to make her let go. But I couldn't. Finally, I managed to ram the high heel of my shoe down on her foot. She swore a horrible string of curses at me, but she didn't let go.

She and Gayle were dragging me farther and farther away. They took me through the trees and down the hill to the shore of the lake. My dress caught on bushes, and I kept stepping on it and hearing it rip.

I was sobbing hysterically by the time we got near the shore. There were cars parked there, three of them, and I almost fainted with relief.

"Help!" I managed to scream. "Oh, please, somebody, help me!"

The people in the cars heard me. I saw their faces looking. But nobody moved.

"Need a hand Jenny?" a girl called out.

Jenny and Gayle always hung out with the group! The three cars were full of them. They were the tough girls from school, and older ones, too. I saw some boys with them, and they were laughing. "Hey, Jenny!" one of them yelled. "Show us what she's got that you haven't got!"

Jenny and Gayle were hitting me and slapping me and kicking me, forcing me to keep moving ahead of them. I was so hysterical from terror; I collapsed on the ground. They picked me up, rough and cruel, and shoved me past the cars. I saw the leering faces of the boys inside. One reached out and grabbed at me. He caught the top of my dress and ripped it. I screamed, but Jenny snapped, "Keep moving, you sneaky little tramp!"

"Take it off!" another boy yelled, All of a sudden, I heard all of them chanting that and clapping their hands. "Take it off! Take it off!"

Jenny and Gayle dragged me over the sand to a breakwater. They yanked so hard at my arms, I thought sure they'd break. They kept dragging me until we were almost at the end, out where the water was deep.

"Let me go! Let me go!" I begged.

"Not yet," Jenny sneered. "Not just yet!"

Then, without warning, the two of them yanked at my dress and the material tore in their hands. They ripped it right off me! I screamed and fought and tried to push them away, but I was too weak and dizzy from panic. They kept on tearing my prom gown. Finally, they ripped it.

"Hey, everybody, take a look at the queen of the prom now!" Gayle yelled.

All of a sudden, the headlights of all three cars went on. The lights were blinding. Gayle and Jenny pushed me so I was standing right in front of the lights. I was screaming and sobbing, but it sounded more like moaning. I was sure I was going to faint, and I was glad. I hoped I'd die and never come to again.

Then, through the haze I was caught up in, I heard a voice say: "Push her in! Let's get out of here!"

Gayle laughed, and Jenny grabbed my hair and jerked my head back. She spit right in my face. Then, before I knew what was happening, she gave me a push off the edge of the breakwater into the dark lake.

The water was icy cold. It shocked the dizziness right out of me. I felt myself going down and down, and I started fighting. My mouth filled with water and my ears were roaring.

Gasping, I finally broke to the surface. Even though I was nearly dead from terror and exhaustion, I managed to swim a couple strokes until my head hit the pillars of the breakwater. I got hold of one of them and hung on. I put my head against the slimy wood, panting and gasping, sobs choking my throat. I was too weak to try to get out of the water or to swim to shore. I didn't know how long I'd have the strength to hang there, but I couldn't move.

It was dark and quiet, except for the lapping of the waves and my hoarse sobbing. I knew Jenny and her group were gone. In the distance, I could hear the music of the prom. It was very faint, like a dream. I couldn't stop my sobs. I felt my hands slipping on the wet wood. I couldn't hold on anymore.

I heard feet pounding on the breakwater, and all I could think was that it was Jenny coming back. Then I heard a voice, broken and sobbing and shrill with terror. I could hardly recognize it at first.

"Jasmine! Jasmine! Where are you?" it called. It was Ray!

Somehow, I found the strength to call out his name. Then he was leaning over the edge, stretching out his hands to me. I reached up, but I couldn't reach him. I fell back into the water, then tried again. Our fingertips just touched.

He leaned over farther, dangerously far, and finally our hands locked. I felt him pulling me out. The air was cold. I was shaking. But I was too scared and sick to be ashamed. The rough planks scratched my skin, but I made it. Ray was crying.

"I saw your clothes. I found your flowers halfway down here," he said. "I thought you were killed, Jasmine! Oh, God, God—" And he couldn't say any more.

He covered me with the ripped pieces of my dress, and then he put his jacket around me. I just lay there, sobbing and shaking.

"I'm going for help," he said, and his feet pounding down the long breakwater were the last sounds I heard before I fainted. . . .

An ambulance came and took me to the hospital, but I was released that same night. I had to tell the police what had happened, and the newspapers got hold of the story and made a big thing of it. I was just sick, having everyone know.

I had to file a complaint against Jenny and her group. Gayle and Jenny and some of the others were in serious trouble. All of them had previous records, and the judge sent them to correctional schools.

The scandal kept growing. I was so ashamed. Most of all, I hated what it was doing to Mom. The whispers were bound to touch her, too, and she'd always been so proud of me.

She said I wasn't to blame in any way, but her eyes looked so hurt and confused. She stood by me, of course, and her love never wavered. But I knew her trust in me would never be the same.

It was almost as bad when I had to face the kids at school the next week. Ray stood up for me, and no one dared to say a nasty thing about me when he was around. But there were times when he wasn't around. Times when I was alone and had to take it and still keep my head up.

The stories about me got worse and worse. They weren't true, but they spread like wildfire. I was in tears by the time I got home each day.

"They'll forget, honey," Mom said. "Every day it will be easier. But, for now, you have to live it down courageously. "

She was right—about living it down, I mean. And Ray is helping me so much. Both of us know now that you have to pay for every foolish thing you do. If he hadn't had the drinks that time at the lake . . . if I hadn't thought it was so important to go to the prom. . . .

But all that's over now. And someday soon, we'll be able to forget all that's happened.

THE END

MOM'S A SNOOP

This is my lucky day, I thought as I hurried down our street.

A water main break at our high school got us an early dismissal, and I could hardly wait to get home and turn on my computer. I'd found a great website the night before where teens could ask questions and discuss anything dealing with sex. It was a subject I didn't care to talk about with my parents.

Most of my friends had already been with a guy, so I didn't feel comfortable talking to them, either. I didn't want them to know how inexperienced I was. I'd been dating Neil for almost three months and he'd been pressuring me to "prove my love."

So far we'd not gone beyond kissing and touching. But I'd be seventeen in less than two months and Neil was already talking about how we'd "celebrate" my birthday.

My tennis shoes were muddy from walking through the muck outside our school, so I slipped them off at the door and headed upstairs. With any luck, Mom would be busy in her downstairs office and I could get online and fire off some questions before she knew I was home.

I felt almost guilty for what I was planning because Mom always told me I could come to her with any questions or concerns I had—and I usually did. But I just couldn't talk to her about this. Our parents were raising my kid sister and me in a church that condemned premarital sex. They would be totally against me having sex on my seventeenth birthday—or any time before marriage. It wouldn't matter to them how out of place I felt with my peers for still being a virgin.

That's why I could hardly wait to get back on this new website and ask all the questions I had about sex. I knew so little and I didn't want Neil to take advantage of me. I had to know what I was getting into before I made a decision whether or not to go ahead and do what he wanted.

When I started down the upstairs hallway, I was surprised to see my bedroom door open. I always closed it when I left for school and Kelsey, my kid sister, was forbidden to go in there without my permission. Besides, I thought only the high school had an early dismissal today.

My heart started pounding as I approached the open doorway. I'm not sure what I expected to see there, but when I looked in, I couldn't have been more shocked if a burglar had been standing there. I stood in mute disbelief as I watched my mother going through my desk drawers. She had obviously gone through several already, as two were still open, and she was leafing through a folder where I kept cards and notes from my friends and other personal stuff. The folder was clearly marked "Personal" and "Keep Out!" as a precaution in case Kelsey decided to go snooping.

Instead it was Mom who had invaded my privacy.

My shock gave way to anger as I stormed through the door. "Mom, I can't believe you'd stoop so low as to go through my drawers and read my personal, private stuff."

I'd startled her and for a moment she just stared at me, her hand at her throat. "Abby, what are you doing home?"

"I'm not answering you until you tell me why you're going through my things."

Her demeanor instantly changed and she crossed her arms and glared at me.

"Don't you take that tone with me, young lady. You are sixteen-years-old and I have a perfect right to make sure you're not into anything you shouldn't be. From the little I've read of these notes, I'm not sure I want you associating with Sonia and Camilla. Girls who boast about having been to bed with a boy at sixteen are not people I want you hanging out with."

"Mom, they've been my friends since first grade. It's not my fault that they decided to do what most kids in our class have already done."

She shook her head and I honestly think she had tears in her eyes. But I was too angry to care. Suddenly, she came and put her arm around my shoulder. "Oh, Abby, if only your friends understood why sex before marriage is so wrong. Not only is it wrong, it's dangerous. You know the possibility of disease is a real threat and people, including young people, are dying of AIDS. Not to mention the possibility of a pregnancy."

"My friends use condoms, Mom. They're not totally stupid."

She took her hand from my shoulder and sat down on the edge of the bed, still holding my folder. "Sweetheart, don't you understand, it's not just about protection. There's so much more to it. And there's more to love and intimacy than just having sex. At sixteen you just aren't mature enough to know about such things. You and your friends can't possibly know about true love, because you don't know enough about yourselves yet—what you want out of life or what you want in a partner. If you give in now to your desires or to the pressures of your friends, you can't really know if you're in love, infatuated, or just trying to fit in."

Mom reached up and brushed the hair from my face. "Abby, please don't be in a hurry like your friends. Date different boys. In time, you'll know when you've met someone truly special. Then, if you take the time to learn everything about him, falling in love and getting engaged will be the most natural thing in the world. And as you grow closer, if you refrain from making love, your wedding night will truly be the most wondrous night of your life—just as God planned it for you."

Mom's speech just made me angrier. It's not like it was the first time she'd said it and it didn't take away what she'd done. "Mom, I've heard this all before. It doesn't change the fact that you've been snooping in my private things, and that stinks. It's just not fair."

"Abby, it may not be fair, but as a parent, I want to protect you. So many kids are into drugs and sex and God knows what else—"

I cut her off before she could finish. "I've never done drugs or had sex or anything else bad. I've never given you or Dad any reason not to trust me. You do not have a right to come in here and go through my things."

"As long as you are living in our home, I have every right to do what I think is best for you."

"What's that mean? Do I have to move out to get some privacy?"

Her eyes widened and she stood abruptly, the folder falling to the floor, spilling its contents across the rug. "Move out? You're sixteen years old."

"I'll be seventeen next month."

We stared at each other and suddenly I realized that I'd done something I'd never done before. I'd yelled at my mother and practically threatened to move out of the house, which I had no intention of doing.

"You are not considered an adult in this state until you turn eighteen. Until then, you will do as your father and I say." Her words were angry and when she finished, she walked out of my room.

My heart was pounding. I'd never heard such anger in my mom's voice before. I started to feel guilty, and then glanced down at all my personal notes and papers spread across the floor. As I bent down to pick them up, my own anger flared again, wiping away any guilt I felt. I'd never given Mom and Dad any reason not to trust me. Mom had no right to come in my room and go through my things.

As I finished gathering everything back into the folder, I silently thanked God that she hadn't found my diary. I'd written in there what Neil was planning for my birthday. Realizing I'd just thanked God for that, I couldn't help but feel guilty again. I was a good person and went to church every Sunday and prayed every day. I knew God did not approve of what Neil wanted to do. I wasn't even sure I wanted to do it. But I did feel left out when my friends talked about sex. When Neil kissed me or touched me, I did feel a tingle deep inside my body. I couldn't help but wonder what it would be like to make love with him, the way a man and woman made love.

With that thought in mind, I shut my bedroom door and locked it before turning on my computer. I got to the website for teenagers and plugged in my first question.

Is it wrong to have sex with your boyfriend when you're seventeen years old?

My question was answered with another question. The words flashed across the screen. Do you want to?

My answer was an honest I'm not sure.

That simple beginning turned into some very frank talk about sex and about a girl's first sexual experience. A lot of it was similar to Mom's comments, mostly about not being ready.

For the next two weeks, I "talked" to a person on this website named Tristan. He became a mentor to me, answering every question with more honesty and frankness than any of my friends had. And he told me a lot more than my parents ever had.

Each night I'd write in my diary about my feelings during these sessions and each day, I could hardly wait to get home and "talk" to Tristan again. He seemed to understand every doubt I had. He told me the more I knew, the less afraid I'd be to take that final step.

By the third week, I was dreaming of this man who had all the answers I needed, a man who understood me, a man who wanted to help me.

I knew the feelings I had when talking to him were stronger than any feelings I'd ever had for a boy, even for Neil. In a way, Mom was right. Getting to know a man was very important. And Tristan wanted to get to know me better, too.

I think I'm falling in love with you, he wrote one day. Could we meet somewhere?

I couldn't believe the thrill that went through me when I read those words. And the thought of meeting him set my heart to racing. I answered simply and honestly. I'd like that.

He wrote back that he'd make the arrangements for our meeting the following Friday after school. He would give me the details the next day.

My diary entry that night was full of the possibility of love that awaited me when I met Tristan. As I tucked my diary between the mattress and box spring of my bed, I could almost feel his arms around me. A delicious, tingly feeling spread through my body and I suddenly knew age had nothing to do with love. I had no doubt that I loved this man I'd never met.

The next day I barely got through my classes. All I could think about was meeting Tristan on Friday. I was anxious to get home and find out his plans for us.

At last the school day was over. Sonia and Camilla came up to me as I was closing my locker. "Hey," Sonia said, "we're headed over to the ice cream shop for a sundae, do you want to come?"

"Nah, not today," I answered.

"Come on, Abby," Camilla said. "You haven't done anything with us for weeks. We're beginning to worry about you. Even Neil called me to ask if you found another boyfriend."

I hoped my face didn't betray me as I answered, "I've been at home studying every night. Where would I have found another boyfriend?"

"Neil said you barely talk to him when he calls and that your last date was two weeks ago," Sonia said.

"I explained to him that my mom was cracking down on me. She's worried that I'll do something stupid like go to bed with him."

"Well, you were thinking about it, weren't you?" Sonia asked.

"I wasn't . . . Neil was."

"Hey," Sonia said, "if you're not ready, you're not ready. I've been having fun doing it, but don't let him talk you into something you don't want to do."

"Believe me, I won't."

"Okay," Camilla said. "Now come to the ice cream shop with us."

I missed spending time with my friends. A part of me really wanted to go, but then I remembered Tristan was going to let me know his plans for our meeting Friday. The mere thought of him was like a magnet drawing me home to my computer.

"Maybe tomorrow," I finally said. "I have some stuff Mom wants me to do after school today." I felt bad lying to my friends, but wasn't ready to share Tristan with them yet.

"Okay," they both said in unison. "Tomorrow."

I hurried home and tossed my coat on the rack just inside the back door. I didn't even take time to get a snack but went straight upstairs, anticipation making my pulse rate soar. I opened my bedroom door to see Mom sitting on my bed, my diary in her hands.

"Mom, what are you doing reading my diary!" I shouted, racing to the bed and snatching it out of her hands.

She didn't speak for several very long seconds. Her eyes held mine and I could sense her doubt and confusion. Finally, she spoke. "When I read what you've been doing, I called your father. He's on his way home. We want you to show us this website you've been on."

"No. No, I won't."

"Yes, you will, Abby. This man could be dangerous. We have to report this to the police."

"Police? Mom he just answered questions over the Internet."

"He's reeled you in, Abby—hook, line and sinker. I only thank God I found your diary before it was too late. Had you gone through with this meeting, I cringe at the thought of what might have happened to you."

"That's not how he is, Mom. He just wanted to get to know me. I wasn't doing anything wrong." The last words were said in a loud, angry tone for emphasis.

She shook her head, then grabbed the diary out of my hand and walked out of the room without another word. I think we were both surprised to see Kelsey standing in the hallway. Mom's voice changed immediately. "Hi, sweetie. I didn't know you were home already. Come on downstairs and we'll find a snack for you."

Kelsey started to walk away, and then turned and said, "Are you coming, too, Abby?"

"No, Kelsey, I'm not really hungry. You go ahead with Mom." I felt bad for my kid sister. She didn't know what was going on, though she couldn't have helped but hear our angry voices. I just hoped she hadn't heard Mom talking about the police.

My mind was still reeling over that. Mom had read everything. My feelings for Tristan, his declaration of love for me, and she knew the day we were meeting. Dad was on his way home. He was no computer genius, but he could easily find the site on my computer. I had to warn Tristan. I didn't even take time to lock my door. I had to work fast.

I'd just turned the computer on when Kelsey came in. "Mommy's on the phone with Daddy. He called from his cell phone. He's almost home."

"Thanks, sis," I said, giving her a quick hug before she headed back downstairs. I knew it hadn't been easy for her to come and warn me. She was a good kid and normally would never go against Mom or Dad. But we were pretty close—at least we had been before I started on this website. I guess she felt some loyalty to me, too.

There was no time to warn Tristan now. I had to get rid of everything as quickly as possible. Thank God for my advanced computer class. Again I thought of the irony of thanking God for something that was going against my parents' wishes. I couldn't think about that right now, though. I had so little time.

My fingers flew across the keyboard. I went immediately to my Internet options and deleted all my temporary files and everything in my Internet history. Then I zipped into my e-mail and deleted all the messages from both my inbox and my sent items.

Then I dumped everything from my recycle bin . . . just as I heard Dad's car pull into the driveway.

I was just shutting the computer down when Dad stormed into my room. I turned and was shocked when I saw his face. I'd never seen him so angry.

"Your mother never should have left you alone with that computer."

94

In the next instant he was at my desk, yanking out the plug and all the connecting cables. Five seconds later, he lifted the tower up in his strong arms and started to walk away. Without that tower my Internet capabilities were gone and no more e-mail, either.

Dad turned and confirmed my worst punishment.

"We'll talk later, Abby. But as of now, you have no computer privileges and you're grounded for a month. Your mother will take you to school and pick you up after school. You will not go out with your friends and there will be no dating. And you will never go out alone with Neil again after what you'd been planning."

"It was Neil who had the plans, Dad. I was going to make up my own mind. That's part of the reason I got onto that website. So I'd be more educated in what he wanted to do. Then I was going to make my decision."

My father looked at me like he didn't know who I was.

"You went on a website to get 'educated' about sex? What were you thinking, Abby? I thought we'd raised you to know sex at such a young age is wrong. Sex outside of marriage is wrong. And if you needed to be educated, you should have come to your mother or me."

I sighed. "You don't understand. I didn't feel comfortable talking to either of you about this. I couldn't even talk to my friends about it."

"So you went to a stranger on the Internet!" he raged. "I've changed my original punishment. Not only are you grounded for a month, you'll have no friends over, nor will you talk on the phone for that entire month."

"But, Dad, my birthday's next week."

"You'll celebrate it here with your family . . . who, by the way, love you very much. At this moment, we love you more than you deserve to be loved."

"I'm sorry you feel that way, Dad, and I'm sorry I've made you angry. But I haven't done anything wrong."

He shook his head and looked at me with such sadness in his eyes. "Oh, Abby, I'm more than angry. I'm disappointed in you. I'm disappointed in your lack of good judgment. I thought you knew the dangers of the Internet. We've talked about it and you ignored all our warnings."

"Dad, nothing happened."

"Thank God and your mother for that," he said, and walked away.

Even though I'd done nothing wrong, I knew in my heart that I might have been heading for that wrong turn. Come Friday, if I'd met Tristan—the way I felt about him—I'm not sure what might have happened. Tears suddenly sprang to my eyes. What would he think when I didn't come online tonight?

Then I realized what he might do. He might try and contact me, and then Dad would be able to track him down. I went out in the hall and grabbed the phone, taking it into my room and closing the door behind me. I was risking getting punished even more for using the phone, but I had to warn Tristan. Quickly, I dialed Camilla.

"You have to do me the biggest favor of your whole life," I said, talking as softly as possible.

"Sure, what is it?"

I quickly briefed her on my talks with Tristan, my plan to meet him, and my parents finding out.

"Geez, Abby, are you nuts? Going to meet a guy you knew nothing about—"

"I don't need a lecture," I said, cutting her off. "I just don't want him to get in trouble. Neither of us did anything wrong. You have to e-mail him for me."

"Aw, that's asking a lot, Abby. I don't want to get involved with this guy. I could get in trouble, too."

"You won't. Just e-mail him. Tell him I've been grounded and he should not e-mail me or try to get in touch with me. Tell him I deleted all my files so there's no way my parents can hassle him. Then you delete your e-mail, too."

"Abby, if we hadn't been friends all our lives I wouldn't do this, you know."

"But we have been," I said.

"Yeah, we have. Okay, I'll do it but just this once. It's the last favor I do until you start being a friend again."

"That may be a while. I really am grounded and my dad took my computer away."

"Good," she said, surprising me. "Sonia, Neil, and I knew something was wrong with you. You were never around anymore. I'm glad your mom found out. You were really dumb to get involved with somebody on the Internet."

I couldn't believe one of my best friends was lecturing me.

"It wasn't like that," I told her. "He's a really nice guy."

"Well, I'm glad you got busted. Maybe you'll get back to normal now, be the friend you used to be before this Internet weirdo came along."

"Camilla, stop talking like that. He's not weird. You don't know him like I do. We really hit it off and like each other a lot and I know this is going to hurt him. So don't say another word. Just do this for me."

I gave her the e-mail address and hung up, making her swear she'd delete it as soon as it was sent.

A little while later, I risked using the phone again, calling her back to ask if she'd done it. "It's done and deleted," she answered.

That evening was the worst night of my life. We ate dinner in almost absolute silence, except for Mom asking Kelsey about her day at school and Dad telling her she could watch a video after dinner.

Mom and Dad tried for more than an hour to make me give them Tristan's website or e-mail address. I refused.

Mom looked at me with such sadness I had to lower my eyes. "Abby," she said, "we are your parents. We have done nothing but love and care for you from the day you were born. How can you choose this stranger over us?"

"I'm not choosing anybody, Mom. And he's not a stranger to me. We've talked for almost a month. He probably knows more about my feelings and what's inside of me than you or Dad."

I knew that hurt her. I could see her flinch when I said the words. But I got past it by thinking of how much Tristan was hurting, too.

"Abby, your mother and I have always told you we were here for you. We raised you to know that you could come to us and talk about anything. If this man knows more about your feelings than we do, it's simply because you never shared them with us. You chose instead to share them with this stranger, someone who could be preying on young girls as naive as you."

"No! He's not like that. He's kind and cares about me."

Mom sighed and Dad paced. "There's no use talking about this any more tonight. We're all tired and angry. Maybe if you go to your room and think about this some more, you'll come to realize that your mother and I are right. That we want to protect you from harm. When you understand that, we can talk again. You will eventually tell us who this man is, Abby, because the police need to know about him. No matter what you think, he had no business making plans to meet a sixteen-year-old girl without her parents' permission."

"If I'd told you, would you have let me go?"

"Of course not," he said. "There can be no good coming of a man who meets young girls via his website."

It had been a long, fruitless talk. Dad was right. I was tired and angry and couldn't make them understand no matter how hard I tried. "Can I go to bed now?" I asked.

"Yes . . . and be sure and pray about this, Abby," Mom said. "You've always trusted the Lord as you were growing up. Trust Him now, too."

I went upstairs, changed into my pajamas, and curled up in bed. But I didn't pray. I couldn't. All I could think about was what Tristan had thought when he got that e-mail from Camilla. It felt strange not to "talk" to him as I had every night for almost a month. He had infiltrated my every waking thought—and my dreams, too. When we'd exchanged photos, I remember thinking he looked remarkably plain for having such a dynamic personality. Yet, the more I got to know him, the better looking that photo became. Because Tristan was so special inside, it made him look good on the outside, too.

I cried myself to sleep that night, missing him and missing my parents, too. Neither of them had come in to say good night for the first time that I could remember.

The soft knock on the door the next morning woke me as sunshine streamed through my window. "Come in," I said, rubbing the sleep from my eyes.

It was Mom and she looked bad. She had dark, puffy circles under her eyes and she was pale. I could tell she hadn't slept much.

She came over and sat on the bed beside me. "Abby, you were asleep when I came in to say good night last night. I felt bad that I'd waited so long because no matter what's happened, your dad and I love you very much. We want you to know that."

"Mom, I keep telling you, nothing happened."

She nodded. "I know that and I thank God for it. But that's not what I meant. I was talking about Dad taking away your computer and grounding you. We've done that because we love you and care about you."

"That's why you read my diary, too? Because you love me?"

Mom sighed deeply. "Yes, that was an act of love, even though I'm sure you think of it as an invasion of your privacy."

"Yes, I do, Mom. That's exactly how I feel. A diary is a person's private thoughts, not meant for anyone else's eyes."

"I didn't set out to read it," she said. "I was turning your mattress, like I do every spring and fall, and the book fell out open on the floor. When I went to pick it up, I couldn't help but see the name Tristan, and soon I found myself reading about this man that I'd never heard of. It frightened me, Abby. But I also felt God had led me to read that page. Otherwise you'd be meeting this man tomorrow and I can't even bear to think of what might have happened to you."

"Oh, Mom, we're never going to see this the same way. I know Tristan meant me no harm. He just wanted to meet me."

"Abby, if you don't come to understand the danger you might have been putting yourself in, we are going to be at a stand-still here. Your father will never allow you to get on the computer again."

It was my turn to sigh. "Okay, Mom. I'll think about it more later. I have to get ready for school now."

The next two weeks passed agonizingly slow. Without my computer and being grounded, I had nothing to do but read or watch television. I thought about Tristan constantly, wondering if he was thinking about me. Without my computer, I couldn't even look at his picture and had to close my eyes tight to try and remember how he looked.

Even my seventeenth birthday wasn't much fun. Mom and Dad

would not relent. I wasn't allowed to have friends over for my birthday, not even my two best friends.

I still had my favorite chocolate cake, but it didn't taste nearly as good as usual. I also got a new outfit and a CD I'd been wanting and Kelsey made me a funny birthday card. But Mom and Dad were still not happy with me. I could feel their disappointment hanging over me as heavy as a thundercloud. I took my CD up to my room and listened to it, but didn't really enjoy it as much as I might have if things had been better between my parents and me.

Kelsey came in before she went to bed to wish me a happy birthday again.

I thanked her and gave her a big hug.

"It wasn't really a happy birthday for you though, was it?" she asked with the candor of a seven-year-old.

"No, not really. But I loved your card and that hug. And things will get back to normal soon, I think."

"Good. I don't like Mommy and Daddy looking sad and I don't like the way you've been acting. I want my old sister back."

I gave her another hug and then went to her room and tucked her in bed. I even read her a story, something I hadn't done in a long time.

And later that same night, for the first time in a while, I prayed. It felt good.

I would've liked to tell Mom, but wasn't ready to take that step yet. I was still very hurt about her reading my diary. I felt like she'd violated something really precious. I could no longer put down my thoughts on paper. She'd taken that special, personal privilege away from me.

It was about ten days later that I woke up to hear animated talking downstairs. I could hear the television news on, too, and wondered if something major had happened. I pulled my robe on and went down to the living room. Mom and Dad were both looking at the television and talking at the same time.

"What's wrong?" I asked. "Did something happen?"

They both turned and looked at me. Mom spoke first. "A fourteen-year-old girl has disappeared. She lives right over in Sea Cliff. Her family has no idea what happened, but her friends said she'd been on the Internet a lot lately and they're checking into that to see if they can find some clue to her disappearance."

Dad looked at me but he didn't say a word. He didn't have to. I knew exactly what he was thinking. "Dad, I wouldn't have disappeared. I know better than to go off with somebody. I would have met him somewhere public. I'm not totally stupid."

He continued looking at me, making me feel uncomfortable. Then he said, "I wonder if that poor girl thought the same thing, Abby."

"The family is asking for prayers for her safe return," Mom said. "I think we should pray together."

So we joined hands and prayed for a fourteen-year-old girl from the next town, a girl we didn't know. We prayed for her safety and for her parents who were going through such a difficult time. It was the first time we'd prayed as a family in a long time and it felt good.

All the talk at school that day was about this young girl who'd disappeared. Several kids in my class knew her, had swum at the community pool with her in the summers, and had seen her at other community events in our town. Sea Cliff was a small town just like Locust Valley and most everyone knew somebody from the neighboring town.

For three days, the missing girl's photo was on the television news and in our local newspaper. It was plain to see that she looked older than fourteen and the police felt that could have been her downfall.

Since none of the girl's clothes were missing and her purse and coat were still in her closet, the police reclassified her disappearance as a kidnapping and the FBI was called in. They took her computer in for analysis to try and learn what might have happened to her or if she'd e-mailed anyone about what she was doing.

It was scary to realize this poor kid's Internet connections might have gotten her in trouble.

I finally had to admit my parents might have been right, and I told them so.

"I know now why you were so upset about what I did," I told them at dinner that evening. "I'm sorry I caused you so much worry. I know it will be a while before you can trust me again, but I hope you will some day."

They both got up and gave me a hug and Kelsey clapped her hands. "Yeah!" she shouted. "Mommy, Daddy, and Abby made up."

After dinner, I went in the kitchen to help Mom with the dishes, Kelsey went up to her room, and Dad went in to watch the news. Mom and I were talking and it was like old times. It was such a relief to have finally gotten past the awful separation between us.

Suddenly Dad called out, "Come here and see this."

Mom and I both rushed into the living room. "They've found her," he said. "Thank God, she's alive."

The kidnapped girl's photo was on the screen, along with an image of a house in another state. We listened as the newscaster told of the FBI finding the man who had been corresponding with this young girl via the Internet. They broke into his house while he was at work and found the girl chained to his bed.

Mom gasped when she heard that and I got a funny feeling in the pit of my stomach. "Oh my God," Mom murmured. "That poor girl."

Then they put the man's picture on the screen and it was my turn to gasp. "It's him!" I cried out. "It's Tristan." I couldn't believe it, but it was. It was the man I'd been going to meet, the man I thought was so perfect.

Dad turned and grabbed both my arms. "What are you saying, Abby? Is that the man you were on the Internet with?"

I nodded, suddenly unable to speak. Tears filled my eyes and if Dad hadn't been holding onto me, I think I'd have dropped to the ground.

In the next instant, Mom had her arms around me and Dad was dialing the phone.

"We have to let the police know," he said. "You may be able to help them nail that sick . . ." He didn't finish his sentence.

While he was on hold, waiting for Sea Cliff's chief of police to come on, he came and put an arm around me, too. I was crying hard by then, unable to believe what I'd seen on that television screen. "That could have . . . could have been me." I sobbed.

Mom was crying, too, and holding me tight.

More details filtered through my sobs. The man had taken her to his home in another state. He was divorced with two children of his own, but lived alone. The girl had met him but had not gone with him willingly. Other details were being held back because of the girl's age.

They showed the police taking Tristan into custody. His face no longer looked kind. When I looked at him, I saw the monster that he was and I thanked God that I had been spared whatever that young girl had gone through.

I hugged Mom and Dad tight. "I'm so sorry. I'm so, so sorry," I said. "I can't believe it. I can't believe that could have been me."

"Shhh," Mom hushed, holding me, brushing the tears from my cheek. "It didn't happen. You're safe with us, sweetheart."

I cried harder, knowing I was safe only because Mom had found my diary.

Dad talked to the police chief and we set up a time for me to be interviewed by the police and FBI.

I went in for questioning the next morning. It wasn't easy telling them about the "relationship" I'd established with that man. I felt so foolish, so stupid. But I told them everything. I had to. I did not want him out on the street ever again. I did not want him to ever take advantage of another young girl.

It's been almost a year since that day they found the girl from Sea Cliff. Tristan has been convicted of kidnapping, unlawful restraint, and transporting a minor over a state line for sexual purposes. He got the maximum penalty of sixty-five years without the chance of parole. Since he was thirty-seven years old that sentence was tantamount to a life term.

I still have nightmares . . . nightmares of being chained to a bed.

When I wake crying, my mother is at my side, holding me, making me feel safe again.

I'll be eighteen next week . . . an adult. But I don't feel grown up. I feel like a lost child, still trying to deal with the horror of what might have been.

I've written this story to try and let the healing begin. To warn young girls and women about the dangers of the Internet. There's much good that can be found from that cyberspace "connection"—as long as you use common sense.

If there are any young women reading this who want to know more about sex, go to your parents, your sister, a good friend. But don't ever "talk" about sex on the Internet.

THE END

MY BROTHER
IS REALLY
MY FATHER!

"Chantal Neville."

As the principal called my name on graduation day, a feeling of pride welled up inside me. I used to have so much trouble in school that nobody thought I'd make it through my senior year. Then I was diagnosed with a learning disorder, and my teachers worked with me on special techniques that helped me learn.

I took the diploma my principal held out to me and shook his hand.

"We're all proud of you, Chantal," he said. "Keep up the good work."

"I'll try, Mr. Bryan," I answered with a grin. I paused at the end of the platform where I knew my dad would be waiting with his camera to take a picture of my big moment. He'd filled dozens of albums with pictures from important days in my life, and he loved to show them off.

"Smile, honey," he whispered, even though he didn't need to. I was so happy I felt like I could smile for days.

After the ceremony, we mingled on the school's lawn with the other graduates and their families, and I said good-bye to all the teachers who had helped me so much. Ms. Ogdon drew me into a warm hug.

"You've come a long way," she said. "Maybe you'll end up back here one day as a teacher."

I laughed. "Thanks for the vote of confidence. But I really think nursing is the right career for me."

I'd discussed my future with Ms. Ogdon a dozen times. She was my favorite teacher, the one who seemed to care the most about how I did. She'd been my English teacher my freshman year and had spent hours of her spare time tutoring me, even after I wasn't in her class anymore. I didn't know why I was lucky enough to have found a teacher who cared so much for my progress, but I was grateful. I would never have been accepted into nursing school without her help.

"You know, Chantal, you're almost like a daughter to me," she said.

I felt tears welling up in my eyes. "Thank you," I managed to say. It wasn't enough, but then I could never fully express how grateful I was. I was relieved to see my dad crossing toward us.

"We'd better head out, honey," he said to me. He nodded at Ms. Ogdon, smiling briefly, before taking me by the elbow and leading me away. I could feel her watching us as we left, so I paused to turn around and wave.

"Aren't we going to wait for Mom?" I asked as he started up the car. She'd come to the ceremony, but I hadn't seen her afterwards.

"She went home early," he said, backing the car out of the parking space. He wiggled his eyebrows at me mischievously. "She's working up a little surprise for you."

"Oh, Dad," I said with a laugh. "You know you don't have to do anything else for me. You've already given me a new charm." I looked down at the tiny, silver graduation cap dangling from the antique charm bracelet I always wore on my left wrist.

Mom and Dad had given the bracelet to me for my eighth birthday. It was too big for my childish wrist at first, but I grew into it. My parents had given me charms to celebrate every major occasion, from the tiny ballet shoe to mark my first dance recital to the star they gave me when I got the first A on my high school report card. I loved my bracelet; I loved to feel like I carried my memories around with me wherever I went.

"And I know you'll have about a million pictures framed as soon as you get your film developed," I continued. "Really, Dad, you guys spoil me too much."

"We can spoil you if we want," he said, his eyes twinkling. "After all, you're our miracle baby."

I laughed and rolled my eyes. Mom and Dad were in their early forties when I was born, so they were older than most of my friends' parents. My brother, who was eighteen when I was born, used to tease me by calling me "The Little Accident." The first time he did it, I'd run to my mom in tears and asked her what he meant.

"Accidents aren't always bad things," she'd told me, her gentle hand brushing my tears away from my eyes. "You were a blessing for us. We call you our miracle baby because we were so lucky to be able to have you."

My dad was tapping his fingers against the steering wheel, frowning at the road in front of us.

"What's wrong?" I asked, suddenly worried.

He smiled at me. "Nothing, sweetie. I guess I was just thinking about how grown up my little girl has become. Your mother and I are going to miss you when you're off at college."

"Oh, Dad. We've already talked about this, you know. The school's only an hour away. I'll be able to come back and visit all the time."

He nodded. "You're right, of course. It'll be nice for you to be able to see your old friends. And your old teachers. You seem especially close to Andrea Ogdon."

I looked at him curiously. "That's funny, I didn't know you knew her first name."

"Oh, everyone knows the Ogdons."

"That's true," I admitted. "They're the richest family in town. And Ms. Ogdon's brother used to be the mayor."

"They're certainly rich," my dad said. He was frowning again. My dad was a plumber, and he'd always had sort of a grudge against rich people, especially the Ogdons. "I've done work in most of the houses in this town. And let me tell you, everyone's got the same pipes and the same problems. Their money doesn't make them any better than anyone else."

"But they do a lot to help people, too," I said, eager to defend my favorite teacher's family. "There's the Ogdon Relief Fund to help the homeless, and the Ogdon Wing at the hospital. And goodness knows Ms. Ogdon's done a lot to help me in school. More than anyone else would've."

"I suppose," my dad said.

I frowned, upset that he didn't take my view of things. I would've said more about how much help Ms. Ogdon had given me, but we'd reached home and he parked the car in the driveway.

"Here we are!" he said, facing me with a boyish grin that made him look years younger than he was. "Let's go and see what your mother's got cooking."

I ran up the driveway and into the house.

"Mom?"

"I'm in the kitchen," she called.

I laid my graduation cap and gown in a pile on the back of the couch and then went into the kitchen, eager to see her and show her my diploma. She was standing next to the sink, putting the finishing touches on a beautiful layer cake decorated in pale pink frosting.

"Oh, Mom," I gushed. "It's so pretty."

"Your favorite color." She grinned. "But that's not all."

I expected her to uncover one of the pots bubbling on the stove and show me what delicious dishes she'd been cooking for me, but instead she took me by the hand and led me into my bedroom. A familiar figure stood in front of my desk, his back toward me. "Jude!" I shouted, and ran to my brother. He turned and enveloped me in a big hug. "You said you couldn't make it!"

"Well, if I'd told you I could, I would've ruined the surprise," he said. He grinned down at me. Everyone commented on how much we resembled each other, in spite of the huge age gap between us.

"This is the best surprise ever. You know how much I love seeing my favorite brother."

Usually when I called him my favorite brother he'd laugh and say he didn't have much competition since he was my only brother. But this time he just looked at me, his eyes sad. He opened his mouth as though he had something important to say, but my mom interrupted him before the words came out.

"Lunch is almost ready," she announced. "You two come on into the kitchen so we can eat."

"Mom, I think I—"

She interrupted his words in a firm voice. "Chantal, wait until you see what I've cooked you. I made all your favorite foods. And some of Jude's, too," she called over her shoulder. "We don't see you very often anymore."

"Yeah, how come you don't visit?" I asked. Jude was an electrician in a town that was only a couple of hours away. But it might as well have been in another country; we hardly ever saw him. "Too busy for the old family now, huh?"

"I'll visit you more when you're at school," he promised. "I'll take you out to dinner sometime. I've heard college food can be pretty bad."

"I know I'll miss Mom's cooking," I said as we all sat down at the table to eat.

I felt uneasy, at first, filled with the nagging thought that something was wrong. I didn't know what was bothering me; maybe it had something to do with the strange way my brother had acted. I knew there was something unusual in the air. I just didn't know what it was. But after a few minutes of joking with my family and talking about happy memories we'd shared at that same table over the years, my doubts vanished. I decided I was just overtired. I'd had a long and exciting day, so it wasn't unusual for me to be a little bit edgy.

Jude leaned back in his chair and gave me a curious look. With one of his eyebrows raised he asked me, "Think you can handle one more present?"

"I don't need any more, that's for sure, but you can give me one if you really want," I said, and we all laughed.

Jude walked over to the fridge and pulled out a bottle of expensive champagne.

"I got you this so we can toast to your future success," he said.

"But I'm not old enough to drink yet," I teased.

"It's okay, honey," Dad said. "We won't turn you in."

My brother uncorked the bottle and poured us each a glass in the fancy goblets my mom saved for special occasions. I could only remember them being used once before, when I was a kid.

"This must've cost you a fortune," my mom chided. "I hope you're not this extravagant all the time."

"I'm careful with my money," my brother replied. "Besides, we're allowed to treat ourselves sometimes, you know. Just because we don't own half the town like the Ogdons doesn't mean we can't have the best."

"Jude," my dad said, a warning tone to his voice.

"Let's toast," Jude said. "To Chantal and her future success."

"To Chantal!" my parents said, and we all took a sip. It was the first time I'd had champagne. It bubbled in the back of my mouth and seemed to tickle my nose.

"Do you like it?" Jude asked, smiling at me.

I nodded. "I have a toast, too. To my wonderful family. Thank you all so much for everything."

We clinked glasses. I noticed my mom had tears in her eyes, and I squeezed her hand.

I only had a couple of glasses of champagne, but it was enough to make me feel tipsy. Probably because I'd never drank alcohol before. I started to help my mom wash the dishes, but she shooed me away.

"I'll take care of everything, honey. Today you get to celebrate. Go do something fun."

"I'm too tired for fun. I think I'll take a nap," I said, rubbing my eyes.

"The champagne must have made you sleepy," she said.

I changed into an old T-shirt and some shorts and laid down. I must have fallen asleep right away. The next thing I knew I was blinking myself awake, the setting sun casting long rays across the foot of my bed. My mouth felt dry, so I got up to get a drink of water.

The kitchen was empty; all the food was put away and everything was scrubbed clean. I smiled. Mom had obviously been hard at work; I knew I had inherited my neat streak from her. I filled a glass at the kitchen sink and slowly drank it, thinking about the party that I'd agreed to go to later that night. Everyone in my graduating class was going to be there. I'd been looking forward to it for weeks.

I heard voices coming from the living room. They were loud, but I couldn't make out any of the words. I pictured my parents and my brother deep in conversation. It had been so long since Jude had visited that they probably had a lot to talk about. I put my glass in the sink and headed down the hallway. I decided I would remind them about the party and then go back to my room to get ready.

But as I walked toward the living room, the worried feeling I'd had earlier returned. I guess it was the tone of their voices, which grew louder the closer I got. I just knew something bad was about to happen.

I paused in the doorway. My mom sat in the armchair, and my dad and my brother were next to each other on the couch. Jude leaned forward, his arms resting on his thighs. His hair was messy, and I knew he'd been running his hands through it the way he always did when he was upset. My mom's eyes were red and she clutched a tissue in her hands. My dad was leaning back with his arms crossed angrily over his chest.

"We have to tell Chantal the truth," Jude said. They hadn't noticed me in the doorway. "She has every right to know."

"Know what?" I asked in a small voice. I wasn't sure I wanted to know whatever it was. I instinctively realized it was sure to turn my life upside down. "What's wrong?" My voice was louder now. "Is someone sick?" My heart started to thud in my chest. That had to be it. One of them was sick and they had waited to tell me until after graduation because they wanted me to be able to celebrate.

"No, honey, we're all fine," my mom said in a small voice. She tried to smile at me, but her lips wavered and she pressed the tissue to her mouth.

"Sit down, Chantal," my brother said. "We need to talk."

"Jude," my dad said, his voice a warning.

My brother just looked at him for a minute. "It's time," he said.

My dad looked away and nodded. "I guess you're right," he said, his voice sounding exhausted.

I sat down on the small sofa next to the door and waited for someone to speak.

Jude cleared his throat and looked at his hands for a moment. Then he looked me straight in the eyes. "Chantal, I'm not really your brother. I'm your father."

I could only blink for a moment, my mind unable to grasp what he was saying.

"But what about—"

"Mom and Dad are your grandparents," he interrupted me.

"Is that true?" I whispered, looking at them. The man I just learned was my grandfather nodded. "I don't understand," I said. "Why didn't you tell me this years ago? Why pretend to be my brother?"

Jude sighed heavily and shook his head. "I was only eighteen when you were born, and my head wasn't right. There was no way I could take care of a baby by myself. Your grandparents decided to raise you as their own, to give you the kind of life I couldn't."

His words swam around in my mind until I grasped onto an important fact he'd just revealed. "By yourself? But what about your . . . what about my mother? Who is she? Where is she now?"

Questions continued to race through my mind. Why had I never met her? Had she abandoned me?

"We met in high school," Jude said. "She was my first love. She was thrilled when she found out she was pregnant, even though her family didn't approve of our relationship. She told me she just wanted someone to love, and to love her back. There was never any question of what to do. She was determined to have you and we were going to get married. Remember that, honey. Your mother always loved you."

I wrapped my arms around my waist, hugging myself as though seeking protection from his words. I still couldn't believe this was real. My graduation cap and gown still lay on the couch beside me, a reminder of the way my life had changed. A few minutes before I'd been a regular teenager, and now I knew my whole life was a lie.

"What happened?" I asked.

"We moved in here," Jude said. "Her family pretty much wrote her off. They acted like she didn't exist. She hardly even noticed, since she was so busy getting ready for you. She made you clothes and read books about childcare. She told me she wanted to be the best mother in the world. We were waiting until after you were born to get married. The only person in her family who still spoke to her was her older sister, who was in college in California. We were waiting for her to come home after her school let out for the summer to be in the wedding."

"And we wanted you to graduate," my grandmother said to Jude. She turned her attention to me as she continued. "He was still finishing up his senior year and working nights at a gas station to save money."

Jude nodded. "Your mother was nine months along and you were due any day when her sister finally came home from school," he said. "She decided it was time to go ahead with the wedding, and they drove around town buying flowers and food and trying to find a minister. The one in town wouldn't marry us. Her family told him they'd switch churches and he'd lose the generous donations they'd been giving him if he dared to marry their daughter to the lowborn plumber's son from the wrong side of the tracks."

Jude's face twisted in pain and his voice was full of bitterness. I knew it was difficult for him to remember the way they'd treated him.

"They drove out to talk to the minister in Wilton," he said, referring to the town ten miles away. "It started to rain on the way back. Andrea was a careful driver, but she wasn't used to driving in bad weather. She took a curve too fast and the car flipped off the road."

Something clicked in my mind when he said the name Andrea, but I was too engrossed in his story to let it sink in.

"I was the one who found them," he said, his voice breaking. "I was coming home from work and I saw the lights down in the ditch. Andrea was fine, but your mother was unconscious. I pulled her out and drove her to the hospital as fast as I could go. They managed to save you, but . . ." His voice trailed off and he rubbed his face with both hands. "We ended up using the money we'd been saving for the wedding to pay for her funeral."

My eyes filled with tears and I looked up at the ceiling, willing myself not to cry. Not yet, anyway.

"What was her name?" I asked as soon as I'd recovered.

"Talia," he answered. "Talia Ogdon."

That's when it all clicked. "You mean Andrea Ogdon is really my aunt?"

Jude nodded. "I didn't know you knew her," he said.

I laughed bitterly. "She was my teacher. She spent hours giving me special tutoring. Now I guess I know why. She felt guilty about what happened."

"Please, honey, don't be angry," my grandmother said. "We tried to do what was best."

"What was best? You lied to me! You kept me from knowing anything about my mother, not even her name."

"We just wanted you to be happy," my grandfather said. "We tried to raise you in a loving home with everything you could ever want."

"That's right. Everything I could ever want except for the truth." I rose and rushed out of the room, blindly flinging the front door open.

"Where are you going?" Jude called. "Chantal, come back!"

I started to run, trying to get as far away from them as I could. My feet pounded against the sidewalk, my breath coming faster and faster. I don't know how long I ran, but when I finally stopped to catch my breath I was standing in front of the convenience store on the other side of town. An idea came to me, and I went over to the pay phone to look up an address in the phone book.

I knew the street she lived on, but I'd never been to her house. It occurred to me that she might not be there, and I decided I'd stay for days, if I had to, to see her and talk to her. Luckily her car was in the driveway. I rang the doorbell and waited.

"Chantal?" Ms. Ogdon asked when she opened the door. She could tell by the expression on my face that something was wrong. "Chantal, what is it?"

"They told me."

That's all I had to say. She held the door open wide and beckoned for me to come inside. We walked into her living room and sat down. I was too upset to notice any of the details of her house.

"I knew they'd tell you eventually," she said softly, more to herself than to me.

"You knew all this time, and you never let on."

"I couldn't," she said, looking into my eyes. "Your grandparents made me promise to keep quiet after you were born. They were going to raise you as their own. They didn't want you to know the unhappiness that surrounded your birth."

"You mean they didn't want me to know the truth," I said bitterly.

"And besides," she continued, "even if they hadn't asked me not to tell, I'm not sure I would've been able to. I'm responsible, Chantal. I'm responsible for your mother's death." Her eyes filled with tears and she looked down at her hands. My heart softened a little, but I was still angry and confused. I couldn't believe everyone I cared about in my life had fooled me all these years, keeping me in the dark about who I really was. I felt betrayed.

"What was my mother like?"

She looked up at me, love lighting up her face. "She was the best person I've ever known. She was always so loving, ready to help anyone who asked. When she got pregnant with you, there was never any question in my mind that she'd keep the baby. She'd looked forward to becoming a mother her whole life."

"Jude mentioned that her family didn't like him," I said, remembering what he'd told me.

"Yes, that's true," she confirmed with a frown. "The Ogdons were always a prominent family in this town. Our parents had hoped that Talia would marry a rich doctor or lawyer. Your dad didn't measure up to their standards."

I drew myself up proudly, ready to leave.

"They're not my standards," she said quickly. "Sit down, Chantal. I'm just trying to explain what happened."

I nodded and returned to my seat.

"My parents were snobs," she said simply. "They weren't able to look past the fact that your dad is a plumber's son and see what a fine person he is. It broke Talia's heart when they threw her out and refused to speak to her anymore, but she never reconsidered the choice she'd made. She was loving enough, or naïve enough, to imagine they'd change their minds eventually, even if it was years after you were born."

"Are they still alive?"

"They died a few years ago," she said. "My dad—your grandfather—had a heart attack. He was gone by the time the paramedics arrived. And my mother passed away about a year ago. I hadn't spoken to either one of them in years, not since they disowned my sister."

"So my mother was wrong," I said. "They never did try to meet me, or even to find out anything about me."

"They were proud people, Chantal. And part of me thinks Talia might have brought them around eventually. She was always their favorite."

We sat quietly for a minute.

"Would you like to see a picture of her?" she asked.

I nodded eagerly, my heart starting to pound in my chest. I'd only known about her existence for a few hours, but I already wanted to learn everything I could about my mother.

"Here she is," Andrea said, handing me a framed portrait. "You resemble your dad, but you've got some of her, too. Especially your smile. The first time I saw you, you reminded me of her so much." Her voice broke and she wiped a tear away from her eye.

I stared at the picture of my mother, taking in every detail I could. She looked friendly and full of happiness, the kind of person who'd laugh a lot. I wished I could've met her, just once.

"I have some more pictures," Andrea said, sitting next to me on the couch. She grabbed a photo album off a nearby shelf and we began to flip through the pages. I was there for hours, listening to her stories about my mother and the childhood they'd shared. It was nearly midnight by the time she dropped me off at my house.

"Would it be okay for me to visit you again? To hear some more of your stories about her?" I asked before I got out of the car.

"Of course," she said, her voice soft. "I am your aunt, after all. I hope you'll come over whenever you want, and I hope that someday you'll be able to forgive me for all that's happened."

I knew she was talking about the accident.

"It's not your fault," I said, putting my hand over hers.

She looked at me uncertainly. It would take a long time for me to be able to help her let go of the pain and guilt she'd been carrying around all those years. I gave her a hug.

"Thank you, Aunt Andrea."

She gave me a grin through her tears. I took the picture of my mom she'd given me and walked into the house. I'd half expected my family to be sitting in the living room just as they were when I'd left, but the room was empty. I saw a light on in the kitchen and peered inside. Jude—my father—was sitting at the table by himself.

"Hey, Dad," I said softly. He looked up at me, surprised, and managed a small smile.

"Are you still mad at us?"

I sat down at the table next to him and shrugged. "Not as much as I was. You guys did what you thought was best."

"We were worried sick about you when you ran out like that, you know."

"I know. I'm sorry. I went to Ms. Ogdon's house. I mean, Aunt Andrea's house." It still felt strange to think of her as my aunt. "Look, she gave me this picture." I handed him the photograph of my mother.

"She was beautiful," he said. "The most beautiful person I'd ever known. I've got some pictures of her at my house. I'll have to bring them out to you."

"Maybe I could visit you there," I suggested. "I think it's time I got to know you better. You are my dad, after all."

112

"Nothing would make me happier," he said.

I'd always known graduation day would be one of the most important days in my life, but I'd never suspected the way it would change things. It took a long time to recover from the shock of learning my whole life had been a lie, and that no one was who I thought they were. I still don't think it was right for my family to deceive me, but I did have a happy childhood, just like they'd wanted me to. I guess it didn't really matter if I called Jude my brother or my dad. The love we shared, as a family, was the same either way.

THE END

SEX WITH
MY TEACHER
Put me at the head of my class!

"Look who's back in pretty good shape," Doug Marshall said to his buddies as I approached them.

To make sure I got the drift of his message, he drew imaginary curves in the air. I tried to ignore him, but as I passed he grabbed my bra strap through my blouse and gave it a snap. I didn't know which hurt more from the sting, my back or my pride.

All the kids in the hall, including the girls, thought this was a colossal joke. Embarrassed and wishing I had a hole to crawl into, I could only manage a weak, "Leave me alone, you creep!" which only seemed to make matters worse by bringing on a new round of laughter. My mortification was now complete.

I fled from the scene only to practically knock down another guy who snapped at me, "Hey, what's your problem?"

That was the highlight of my first day back to school. And the days following weren't much better.

I was a fourteen-and-a-half-year-old girl trapped in an adult body, surrounded by a school filled with hormonally charged, immature boys who lived and breathed only sex. My misfortune was to have developed more quickly than most girls my age. According to my mom, it was the same way with her and her mother. Sort of a family trait, I guess.

I couldn't believe how she'd speak about it with pride, since I didn't find it much of a blessing, especially when all the boys at school gawked at my breasts. Because of my full figure, I wore loose clothing and tried to look younger by not wearing any makeup, even though the other girls did.

As much as I tried to avoid Doug and his friends, they seemed to always be in my face, making my days at Sterling High a living hell. We were in some classes together, which didn't help, either. The fact that the school was small just made things worse. Just because they were on the football team, they thought they deserved special privileges and acted like they owned the place. Doug, especially, thought that every girl should fall at his feet and be crazy for him. Okay, he was pretty good-looking and had a great body, but he was still a jerk. And that said it all.

Basically, all my troubles with Doug Marshall began last year.

Mom and I had just moved here after Dad had run off with his secretary. Mom's company offered her more pay if she transferred, so we ended up in this small town. My first day at school last year turned out to be a warning of what was to come.

I remember being nervous walking to my first class that day. Suddenly, this big guy blocks my path and says, "Hiya, babe. New here?"

"Yes," I said, still somewhat startled. He had bright eyes that seemed to make me feel even more uncomfortable. Then I realized why. They acted like x-rays peeling away my clothes. He didn't seem to be budging and if he didn't get out of my way, I'd be late for class.

"Please let me pass."

"What's your hurry? It's your first day. They always cut you some slack."

"I really don't want to be late."

His eyes narrowed. "You don't think talking to me is important?"

"I didn't say that."

"But that's what you meant."

I shook my head and pushed by him with all my might. I thought I heard him mutter something not very nice. Four periods later at lunch, he sat down next to me with three other guys. I was so nervous that I nearly spilled my milk all over my sweater.

"So, you gonna tell me your name or not?"

"Melody."

He raised an eyebrow.

"Melody Hawkins."

"Well, Melody Hawkins, I'm Doug Marshall and this is Joey Cooper, Brad Thompson, and Ricky Winters. We're the official greeters of Sterling Junior High."

"You don't talk much, do you, Melody Hawkins?" Doug said.

I shook my head. I really wanted him to go away and take his friends with him. The other girls at a nearby table seemed to be watching what was going on quite intently. Did this guy do this with everyone new, or was it just me?

"Maybe we can get to know one another better. Wanna hang with me on Saturday?"

"No," I said, shaking my head for emphasis.

"Why? Got a boyfriend?" he asked as he rubbed my hand.

I pulled my hand away as if I'd been burned. He didn't like that one bit.

"You're going to regret this. Nobody turns a date down with me."

That's how it all began and now I see how much he meant it—the regret part. The more I said no, the more he annoyed me. The weird part was that the other girls thought I was crazy. I just didn't get it.

Why would anybody want to be with such a conceited jerk?

I thought it all would've ended over the summer vacation. We were starting a new school and there'd be more girls for Doug and his crowd to annoy. Boy, was I ever wrong. Doug soon found himself an important member of the varsity football team, never losing his hero status or his ego.

Two days before the big game against our school's rival, Doug cornered me at my locker.

"Hi, sweetcakes."

"Don't call me that."

"Well, no one has a pair of buns like you have," he said, putting his hand on my backside.

"Don't touch me!" I said, slapping his hand away.

To my surprise, he boldly grabbed my breast, chuckling. "Just wanted to see if they were real."

I slammed my locker, wanting to run away. To my surprise, his other hand was there. He roared in pain as the locker closed on his hand, "You broke my hand, idiot!"

"It's your own fault. Now stay away from me!" I said as I fled down the hall.

"I'll get you for this," he shouted and the echo of his voice chased after me down the hall.

The following day, Doug came into school with his hand bandaged. From what I heard, his fingers weren't broken, but very badly bruised. In one slam of a locker, I managed to incur the wrath of the entire school. Nobody knew the reason why it happened. I certainly had no intention of telling anyone. It wouldn't have mattered anyway, since without its star running back, our school had little chance of beating Middletown High in the football game on Saturday.

I had the misfortune of having Doug in my history class. Mr. Barnett, our teacher, was young, handsome, and really cool. He tried to make history more exciting than it's usually taught, which is not too easy, if you ask me.

Halfway through the period, I noticed a note being passed around the room.

I had a feeling it concerned me and I watched as student after student opened it and snickered before passing it on. When it reached the girl sitting next to me, I was able to see what it was. Somebody, probably Doug, had drawn a crude picture of me without clothes. Embarrassed would hardly describe how I felt at that moment.

"Ms. Andretti," Mr. Barnett's voice said, interrupting my thoughts. "Please bring that to me."

Lisa got up and gingerly handed him the slip of folded paper.

"You may sit," he said, after peeking inside. Then, as if nothing

116

had happened, he continued on with the lesson. I guess everyone was waiting and wondering what he was going to do, because the room was totally silent.

When the bell rang, I saw Doug give his friends the V sign, figuring he got away with it.

"Mr. Marshall, Ms. Hawkins, I'd like you both to remain behind a moment, please."

Mr. Barnett glared at Doug. "I'd have to be completely dumb not to know what has been going on in this class."

Doug smirked and that set Mr. Barnett off. "You think this is funny?" he said, throwing the folded note at him. "I doubt if she does."

When he said that, he glanced at me and sent a new wave of embarrassment down my entire body to my toes.

"So, you don't like it. What does it have to do with me?"

"Everything, since I watched you draw it. I also suspect that you probably had that coming to you," he said gesturing toward Doug's bandaged hand.

"Can we wrap this up before I'm late to my next class?"

"You may leave as soon as you apologize to Ms. Hawkins."

Doug started to say something, but thought best not to. Instead, he spat out a most unconvincing, "Sorry."

I'm certain that Mr. Barnett probably felt the apology was the best he could expect from the likes of Doug and let it slide. He allowed Doug to leave with a warning. "I will not tolerate any more of this kind of nonsense in my class. Do you understand?"

Doug nodded.

"Now, get out of my face."

Doug didn't need an engraved invitation. He took off as fast as he could.

After Doug had gone, Mr. Barnett's entire manner changed. He gently tucked his finger under my chin and said quietly, "If Doug does anything to hurt you again, let me know."

"Thank you, Mr. Barnett."

"I suspect there's much more to this, but there's no time to discuss it now. Why don't you come and tell me all about it tomorrow during your study period? I'm usually in my office at that time."

"Thanks."

"See you tomorrow," he said, smiling.

The heavy weight I'd been dragging around suddenly felt lighter. Somebody really cared how I felt. For the first time, in such a long time, I felt good about myself. It took the sting out of being ridiculed by the other students.

I went to Mr. Barnett's office the following day during my study period. Because he was the faculty advisor to the history club, he had his own office with an old sofa, a table, and four chairs. It wasn't much larger than a closet, but it was quiet.

I felt a little uncomfortable at first telling him all about my problems with Doug Marshall, but that quickly passed. I even told him how Doug hurt his hand.

"It's understandable why the boys act the way they do about you."

"It is?"

"Of course. You're a beautiful young girl with an amazing body for your age. Those boys are just too immature."

Day after day I'd find myself spending my study period with Mr. Barnett in his tiny office. We'd talk about my problems and me as well as my schoolwork. My grades began to pick up in all my subjects, and not just history. This pleased my mom very much.

"Whatever you're doing, sweetheart, continue," she'd say each time I handed her something with a good grade on it. "I'm so proud of you."

So I continued to spend my study periods with Mr. Barnett. He didn't talk down to me like I was a child. In fact, the big difference in our ages seemed to melt away when I was there. He didn't mind that I called him Gabe when we were alone. The nicest part of it all was the fact that I always left his office feeling good.

Not before long, Doug Marshall became interested in another girl and soon forgot all about me. After that, the other kids weren't as mean to me. At that point, it really didn't matter anymore, because of Gabe Barnett.

I began to look forward to seeing Gabe and wore clothes that made me look older. I wanted to please him. Often I found myself thinking about him, wishing I were older so we could date. My mother noticed this further change in me and happily thought I was finally settling into the new school. She had no idea that I had a major crush on my history teacher.

Gabe began to say things that made me think he had feelings for me as well. He'd compliment me on my dress or the perfume I was wearing. Sometimes he'd bring me a tiny present whenever I did well on an exam. But nothing prepared me for what happened one day a month or so later.

He'd graded my test right before I came by and gave me a big hug when he showed me my perfect paper. Before I could recover from the excitement of the hug, he kissed me. It wasn't a little peck on the cheek, but a real kiss on the lips that took my breath away. I could hardly believe that it happened.

"I've been wanting to do that for such a long time," he said. "I hope you didn't mind."

Even though he'd caught me off guard, I enjoyed every sensation of the kiss. I shook my head no, but could only stammer, "What if somebody comes in?"

"Don't worry, I locked the door."

My heart nearly exploded with joy. I was right! He did care about me. When Gabe took me in his arms and began to kiss me over and over again, my heart began to beat in triple time. It pounded so, that with each beat I feared it would break clear through my chest. We didn't stop kissing until the period was nearly over.

"I liked doing that, did you?" he asked.

"Yes, very much."

"You mustn't tell anybody about it or else I can lose my job."

"I wouldn't want that to happen."

"Me, neither," he said. "See you tomorrow."

The following day, he asked if I told anyone about the kissing we did the day before.

"Of course not! I can keep a secret."

"Good. I took a big chance."

"Why did you do it if you could be fired?"

"Because I really like you a lot."

"I really like you a lot, also," I heard myself say.

"That's good, very good," he said and smiled.

I felt the warmth of that smile straight through me to my toes. I'd never felt that way before.

"If only you were a little older, people wouldn't raise eyebrows about our feelings toward each other."

"They just don't understand."

"It's a little more than that. You're considered a minor."

"But you don't care about that."

"That's true. I do consider you to be somewhat older than your years, but others won't if they ever caught us kissing. That's why it must remain our little secret."

"We won't ever let them know."

"That means we can't date."

"I understand. I'm happy to spend the little time we have together here."

"Then you'll be happy about the surprise I have for you."

"What? Tell me, please!"

"Saturday, we're going on a picnic to a small park I found."

I was nearly overwhelmed by the excitement and though Saturday was only a few days away, I could hardly wait. My dream of actually being on a date with Gabe was coming true. But was this what I really wanted?

My mom had told me all about sex. She said it was something adults do when they love one another. I also think she meant it was

119

best to get married first in case of accidents and got the feeling that I was one. Where did Gabe and I fit into all this? He was an adult who treated me like one. And I did have the body of an adult. I guess I shouldn't have let Gabe kiss me and certainly should stop going to his office, but whenever I was with him I could hardly say no. I liked myself when I was with him and that alone was enough to keep me coming back.

I told my mom that I was going to the library on Saturday to do a research paper for history.

"Would you like me to drive you over there?"

"No, thanks. It's a beautiful day, so I'd rather ride there on my bike."

"Have fun. I mean, study hard."

"I will."

I was meeting Gabe a block away from the school. He was there waiting for me when I arrived. He jumped out of his car quickly and put my bicycle in the back. When we were both in the car he kissed me, sending little tingles of sensation throughout my body.

"Wait until you see this place."

I could hardly breathe. Between my curiosity and excitement, I was practically going crazy. Luckily, we didn't have to go too far. I understood why Gabe picked it. It was a beautiful spot, secluded from the main road and didn't seem to be visited often.

"Here we are. Our own little place."

"Nobody else comes here?" I asked.

"Not that I know of."

"How did you find it?"

"I happened upon it by accident one day. Come give me a hand with this."

I took the opposite end of the blanket from him and helped spread it out on the grass. He sat down and held out his hand to me. "It's a little too early to eat, but we can if you're hungry."

I shook my head.

"Then scoot over closer."

He was lying on his side with his head resting on his hand. With his free hand he gently traced the outline of my face, making it hot every place he touched. Smiling, he drew my face closer and kissed me. One kiss led to another until we were both gasping for breath.

"You're so beautiful," he said as he kissed my breast through my blouse. It felt so strange. He began to open my blouse, kissing my neck at the same time. I began to feel sensations deep within me that I'd never felt before. They were wonderful and I wanted more.

"So beautiful," he repeated as he touched me.

Then Gabe took off his clothes. I guess he was just as excited about

120

what we were doing as much as I was. The fact that I had such an effect on him gave me pleasure. Then we did it. It was, and yet wasn't, what I expected. I only know I never felt that close to another human being before.

Afterward, Gabe held me in his arms. I felt so at peace. He kissed me.

"I'm sorry that happened," he said.

"Why?"

"It was wrong."

"No, it wasn't. I wanted it, too." I couldn't understand how something that felt so good could be wrong.

"It's a lot more serious than kissing. Not only could I lose my job, I can also go to jail."

"But no one has to know but us two. And I'll never tell."

Gabe was always very honest with me. I guess he wanted me to know what was at stake. Even though it was more of a risk for him, going to jail and losing his job, I'd be gossiped about forever. The fact that he trusted me to keep our secret made me love him even more. But what if somebody found out somehow? There was always a chance.

When Gabe began to kiss me again, all my worries disappeared. Being with him in his safe, strong arms was worth the risk.

In the following weeks, I wanted to be with Gabe more and more.

Unfortunately, because of the circumstances surrounding us, we only had stolen moments together. I couldn't go to his apartment because he lived in a two-family house. We couldn't chance his landlord seeing me. I longed to hold his hand in public and be able to kiss him in front of the entire world. To go to a movie or even have dinner in a restaurant together would be wonderful. But all this was out of the question.

"It's not fair."

"What's not fair?" Gabe asked as I lay in his arms after making love.

"Not being able to be seen together."

"We've gone through this a half-dozen times."

"I know, but I still don't think it's fair."

"Fair or not, that's the way it is unless you want me to go to jail."

"You know I don't."

"Then stop acting like a child, or we'll have to stop seeing one another."

"No!" I begged him. That would be the worst thing. I was in love with Gabe and didn't know what I'd do if he ever said good-bye.

For a while the subject would be dropped, but never forgotten. Gabe often said that time was on our side. When I was eighteen, things would be different. But that was nearly three years away. I feared that in the meantime he'd fall in love with someone closer to his own age.

The school year was nearly over. This meant that Gabe and I could meet at our secret place or even find another, if necessary. It seemed that I thought about nothing else. My entire world revolved around Gabe.

When the last day of school had arrived, I wasn't sad. I'd spent some time with Gabe in his office and made plans to meet him the next day. That night I dreamed of marrying him and having lots of kids.

I woke early the next morning and got dressed. Mom had already left for work, so I had some breakfast by myself. It was almost time to meet Gabe, so I cleaned up the breakfast dishes and grabbed my bike. When I got to our meeting spot, I saw that Gabe hadn't arrived. Usually he was there waiting for me. But after an hour, I knew he wasn't going to come. I wondered where he was, hoping that nothing bad had happened to him. Worried, I rode over to the place where he was staying. I knew I'd promised never to go there, but this seemed to be an emergency.

When I got there, the front door to his apartment was open. I poked my head inside and saw a man painting the walls. The place looked vacant.

"Can I help you?" he asked.

"Yes. I'm looking for Mr. Barnett."

"Sorry, but he's gone back home to New York. Left late last night."

Gone? How could he be gone? He said he loved me. And I loved him. No, something wasn't right. He left without even saying good-bye. I fought to keep the tears forming in my eyes from falling.

"I thought he moved here to live."

The man shook his head. "He told me that this job was only temporary. I think he was waiting for a teaching position back home. I know he hated having to leave his wife and a little girl back in New York."

I thanked the man and ran off just as my tears began to stream down my face. I could hardly breathe. He had a wife and child! I could hardly believe what the man was telling me, yet it must've been true. After all, why else would Gabe leave like a thief in the night, taking my heart and soul with him. I wiped my nose. I felt like a little fool. I'd believed everything he'd said to me. Now it seemed that nothing he'd said to me was true. He merely said the things I wanted to hear and used me. How could I be so stupid?

I'd been so innocent when he came into my life and trusted him. He'd given me my first real kiss and was my first love. My mother always told me how a woman tends to remember those things forever. How would I ever be able to think of either without feeling the pain and shame that he left me with?

I walked my bike down the road a bit and sat down. There was no way that I could go home feeling the way I did. But where could I go? An urge to hurt Gabe the way I was hurting grew within me. Then I realized that I couldn't tell anyone about us and what we'd done together. If I did, though, I'd only be bringing shame to both my mother and myself. She didn't deserve that and I certainly didn't want her to think that I was some kind of tramp, so how could I ever tell her, either? This was one terrible secret that I had to keep to myself. How would I ever be able to do that? I buried my head in my hands and cried. I don't know how long I cried my heart out, but it would've been much longer had a police car not slowed down to see if I was hurt. I hopped on my bike quickly and rode away.

I reached home still feeling awful. The fact that I'd allowed myself to be used bothered me greatly. I wished I hadn't been so naïve. But then again, I was only fifteen. Well, all that innocence was certainly gone for good. I knew all about sex now. So, where did I fit in? There was no way I could go back to being the kid I once was any more than I could be an adult. I felt truly lost.

By the time my mother got home, I'd made myself more presentable. I didn't have much of an appetite and played with my food.

"What's wrong, Melody? Don't you feel all right?" my mother asked.

"I don't know. I guess I'm not really hungry. Can I go lie down?"

"Of course, sweetheart. I'll check on you later."

My mother didn't deserve a kid like me. She worked so hard for the both of us and look what I did. Maybe she'd be better off without me. That was the last thing on my mind before I dropped off to sleep.

I dreamed that I ran away and got a job as a waitress in a diner in another city. I lied about my age so I could get the job. It wasn't the greatest, with the men pawing at me all the time, but it gave me enough money to live on. I'd come home late at night and crash. I seemed to be so tired all the time. But most of all I missed my mom.

In the dream I was able to see her, as if I were looking through a magic window. She cried all the time over me, because she missed me, too. Then she got sick and died. I never got the chance to say good-bye or to tell her how much I loved her. I woke up crying. That's when I realized that I couldn't run away.

I wasn't ready to tell my mother what had happened between Gabe and me, but I knew that I'd be able to one day. Somehow, I felt that she'd find it in her heart to understand. Until that time I had to find a way to get beyond it, even if it took a long, long time. Thanks to my history teacher, I learned a lesson that I'd never forget, but I doubt that I'd be so easily sweet-talked next time.

THE END

Could It Happen To Your Daughter?
DOING HARD TIME
AT 17
For this teen, the nightmare
will not end

Frankie is standing before me, his hands reaching for me, his face troubled. I just want him to kiss me. . . .

I know this is a dream. I am hanging onto that one last dream before really waking up. Any minute now, my favorite music will start pumping out from the pink clock radio in my bedroom. The morning light will brighten the posters on my walls and seep across the piles of clothes on the floor.

Where is that music? I want it loud and rappy with a metallic underbeat that I can draw across my eyes like a veil. My mother will have coffee going in the kitchen. I'll wear my favorite jeans today and my burgundy top with the skinny straps. Stretching and curling up again, I keep my eyes tightly closed. I decide I won't go to school today. I'll get my boyfriend, Frankie, to give me a ride to the mall. But first. . . .

A honking buzzer, an ugly intrusion, jars me fully awake. A man's voice on the loudspeaker announces that we have three minutes until breakfast. We have to make our beds. It's cold. The stale, nauseating smell of the plastic breakfast trays billows up to the cells on the second tier. I open my eyes and remember that I am in jail.

Who would think it could come to this? Frankie is in jail, too, somewhere in the same building but far away, where they keep the boys and men. What did he tell them? Whatever he and his friends said, I'm afraid that's why I'm still here, in the women's section, dressed in murky green cotton scrubs over long johns, waiting and afraid.

I touch my clothes with distaste. They obviously don't use fabric softener here. No clothes of my own allowed. No makeup. No hairspray. Not even a rubber band to make a ponytail. No music. No radio. No television, either, except for a half an hour later in the evening when we can watch the news. Who cares about the news? No friends to talk to. Nothing to do. Hours and hours of nothing to do. There are some old books and tattered magazines on a shelf in one of the interview rooms, but I can't concentrate on reading. I can't concentrate on anything. When will my mother get me out of here?

I'm not a criminal. I didn't do anything wrong. I just rode along with Frankie and his friends and we stopped at this guy's house and there was a fight. I didn't even know what we were there for. And somebody fired a gun and then someone got hurt. Like, killed hurt.

I look in the mirror. My own face shocks me. I look awful. My hair is stringy and my skin is chalky. I am seventeen and I have never been so afraid and so alone in my life. But you can never really be alone here. There is no privacy. And these people are scary. There are women with their teeth knocked out and women with black eyes. There are fifty-two of us—or, rather, there are fifty-two cells. The women come and go. There are a few girls here my age; minors they call us, but most are older, in their twenties or thirties or even older. I don't know what they did. It's not polite to ask that here, I found out. But sometimes people just tell you. In the cell next to me is a beautiful black girl with her hair braided in a hundred little braids. I heard her crying the other night. She told me she misses her baby.

There is one woman with the scariest eyes. She's in here for prostitution. I don't get it. She isn't attractive at all. She acts like she runs the place. The officers all know her and she seems to be pals with several of the other prisoners. I am afraid of these people, but some are nice. That older woman, the one with a barbed-wire tattoo spanning her upper arm, calls me baby girl and she gave me some extra packets of sugar for the gray, disgusting cereal they serve for breakfast.

The guards keep changing. I can't keep them straight. They don't want to hear anything I have to say. They want me to do what they tell me. All they care about is the rules.

"Sure, and this is charm school," one of them joked when I tried to tell him that I'm innocent, that it was my boyfriend's fault, and that my mother is going to come and take me home any minute.

I miss my mother. My mother and I had terrible fights but she cares about me. She was pretty young when she had me, so we're more like sisters than mother and daughter. We wear a lot of the same clothes and sometimes we talk about our boyfriends. She really understands how hard it is. She hasn't been to visit me yet, though. I begged my mother to put money in my account here, so I could buy some lotion and some of those little packets of hot cocoa like the other inmates have, but there isn't any money there yet. Or maybe she has to wait until she gets paid. That's probably it. Or maybe she's still mad at me.

We had a big fight that night, just before Frankie picked me up. She was mad because I took money out of her special hiding place and went shopping. She told me to get a job! But how am I going to get a job without a car, and besides I have to go to school, and what kind of a job would I get, anyway? I know it was wrong to take the money, but I needed some things. Or maybe she's mad because I'm in jail. Like I would go out and get arrested on purpose. But it's Frankie's fault. Doesn't she see that? Anyone could see that. What did he tell them? Why am I still here? There's too much time to think here. This place is a drag.

There is nothing to look forward to but the meals, and the food stinks. You have to do what they tell you here. If you don't, if you give them any trouble, they can lock you in your cell for hours, for days. It is so unfair. There is nothing to do. There is nowhere to go. You can't listen to music or call your friends. You can't make calls at all except collect calls at a certain time of the day.

I think I have a lawyer but I'm not sure. I know that my mother can't afford one, but I thought that the court was supposed to appoint one for me like on television. I don't know how that works. I wonder how long I have to wait.

This is outrageous. I have to get out of here. I can't miss this much school. They tell me I have to go to school here, GED school. Every day this dumpy teacher comes in here with her little plastic case of worksheets. She smiles and says she is glad to see us. Yeah, like there's anywhere we could go to get away from her. And we have to sit there for hours and just work while she helps us. I don't want her help. This is so dumb. No way I'm getting a GED while they keep me away from my own school. I am going to college and I am going to be a lawyer. Now I might really do that—become a lawyer—because I'm so mad. I'll show them. I'll show Frankie. Oh, God, I have to get out of here. I have to.

"Thirty-eight! Tanya! Thirty-eight!" My heart pounds wildly. The officer has shouted my name. It's the young, female cop with the pretty hair. I make my way over to the control desk where the officers sit. She checks my wristband and glances at my face briefly to confirm that it matches the picture on the ID band. How can she even tell? The picture doesn't look anything like me.

"Attorney visit," she tells me and jerks her thumb toward the tiny interview room where a man sits with a briefcase.

Finally!

I put my fingertips to my hair and pull my shoulders back, thinking that if I flirt a little with this lawyer guy maybe he can get me out of here. That's his job, right?

But no. Oh, he's my lawyer all right but he tells me that I'm not getting out right away, not without a whole lot of bail money that my family doesn't have, of course. My trial is set for three weeks away—three weeks?—and that I'll be lucky if I get only three to five years on a guilty plea. Frankie is going to testify against me. I can't believe it. The lawyer tells me not to call his office. They don't accept collect calls. He barely looks at me. He tells me he'll be in touch. I don't even know his name.

The officer orders me back to my cell. There is a precise, metallic click as the guard locks me in from the remote electronic system at the control desk. I flop onto the little bed and pull the shapeless blanket around me. The coarse blanket catches on the plastic bracelet that I, like all inmates, wear around my wrist. The ID picture they took the night I was arrested looks back at me from my wristband. It is starting to get faded, blurry from the water in the shower. The number reads 05G2205. Is this who I am, I wonder, that terrified, blurry face, inmate number 05G2205? Why doesn't my mother get me out of here?

Maybe my mother can't fix it this time. It seems like I don't belong to my family anymore. It seems that I belong to these guards and to these gray walls like I'm one of the plastic meal trays. Three to five years in prison! Sleep. That's the only thing to do. I'll go to sleep and I'll wake up and everything will be okay again.

Won't it?

THE END

14 YEARS OLD
AND LIVING ON
THE STREETS

Main Street ran through the seediest part of town, and it always had a lot of traffic. The pawn shops, tattoo parlors, strip clubs, and bars were all on Main Street between Stanton and Franklin Avenues.

That part of the city was full of crime, corruption, drugs, and sudden violence. Respectable people went out of their way to avoid Main Street. I didn't have that luxury. It was where I lived and worked.

I've been here almost two years, and in that time I've received quite an education, the kind you can't get in school. I've learned where to get a meal when you haven't eaten in days and don't have a dime in your pocket, where to sleep when you have no place to stay, and where to find a job when there are no jobs available. I learned to do what a lot of people much better off than I had failed to do—I learned how to survive.

I work nights at Eighteenth and Main, and I have to wear a uniform—five-inch heels, black hose, a skirt that barely covers my behind, and a blouse open to the navel. I make my living off men who are willing to pay for a little entertainment. Sometimes that entertainment takes place in a roach-infested motel a few blocks away, but most of the time it's in the customer's car. On a good night, I can make two hundred dollars. Not many girls my age make that kind of money. I'm fourteen years old.

It's easy work. All you have to do is what comes naturally. The men drive up and start to chat with the girls on the corner, and then they make their choice. At first I thought the older girls had an advantage because their figures were more developed. Then I discovered that men would pay a premium for a very young girl. A lot of guys think I'm only twelve, and if that's what they want, that's what I am. The customer is always right. I'm a businesswoman.

Maybe you think that's a joke. Maybe you're some big shot with an office and you make important business decisions every day. Well, so do I. Whenever a guy pulls up to the curb and motions to me, I have to make a decision. Is this guy an undercover cop who is going to bust me, or someone who is going to refuse to pay me? Is this a guy who is going to get his satisfaction from quick, impersonal sex, or is he going to get rough? In the two years I've been on the street, five girls I know have been murdered. Their killers have never been caught. Hookers often disappear and when their bodies are discovered it's no big deal, either to the cops or to the general public.

This is not a profit or loss type of business. It's one of life and death, and the only thing you have to rely on is instinct and experience. You have to keep on your toes every day. Some days are better than others.

Perhaps you're wondering how I got into this sort of life. Maybe you're thinking it couldn't happen to you or your children. Well, think again, because it's not that difficult. No matter who you are, or how much money you make, the street is never far away. For a lot of people, it's only a matter of a couple of paychecks.

I was one of those middle-class kids living a sheltered life in the suburbs of a small town. I was eleven years old, and the biggest problem I ever faced was deciding what clothes to wear. When my parents divorced, it was the biggest surprise of my life. Overnight, my cozy little world was turned upside down. Now I had two places to live, and neither of them felt like home.

Every other weekend I went to stay with my dad. He had a tiny apartment in a run-down neighborhood, and my room there was barely big enough to hold the bed. All the time I was there, we had to do things. Whether it was going to the amusement park, picnics, or rides in the country, it all had to be crammed into the weekend. It wasn't like being at home. I felt like a guest who had to be entertained.

At home with Mom, it was the opposite. There never seemed to be anything to do except watch TV. I seldom went anywhere with Mom. "I think your father's got something planned for the weekend," she would say. That was always her excuse. I began to feel like I'd become a burden to both of them.

"Why can't you and Dad get back together?" I asked. We'd all been happy then. We'd been a family.

"Jenna, I've told you this before," Mom said firmly. "Your father and I will never get together again. That part of our lives is over. We have to go on with the future."

If that was what the future was like, it didn't seem very promising. I wanted us to be a family again. I didn't understand why I could only be with my father every other weekend. Maybe he thought I didn't love him as much. If I could show him that I did, then maybe things would be all right again.

I got out the phone book and turned to the city map at the front. It was all shrunk down to fit on a single page, and it was difficult to read the street names and see what labels belonged where. I must've studied it twenty minutes before I figured out where Dad lived.

I checked it a couple of times to be sure. It was a lot farther away than I thought. In the car, it didn't seem like much of a ride. On my bike it would be a lot different. I'd never ridden it more than a few blocks from home. I'd never gone on the busy streets. I'd never gone outside the area I was familiar with.

I cut the map from the phone book and planned my route carefully. I didn't take the shortest path, but the one that would let me avoid the busiest streets. Next, I chose what I was going to take with me. Since the project seemed so immense, I decided to bring enough clothes for a week. I packed my toothbrush, but not any of my dolls. It was going to be difficult enough carrying everything on my bike.

On the top shelf of my closet was a pink piggy bank where I kept all the money people gave me. It held forty-one dollars and eighty-three cents, which seemed like more money than I'd need. I took it all anyway.

It was summer and there was no school. Mom had gone shopping that afternoon, leaving me alone for an hour or so, as she sometimes did. I'd probably be at my dad's place before Mom got home. Loading my things onto my bike, I set out on my journey.

Nothing had gone according to plan. The extra baggage made the bike hard to maneuver, and there were a lot of hills I had to pedal up. Traffic was heavier than I expected. I ended up pushing the bike more than riding it. Some of the streets had similar names, and I kept getting lost. I was tired and hungry.

It wasn't until I saw a letter carrier that I did something sensible—I asked for directions. Once I got my bearings, it only took me a few minutes to reach my father's apartment. As I drew nearer, another problem occurred to me. What if he wasn't home? I couldn't wait too long for him. Mom would be wondering about me.

When I saw my Dad's car on the street, I felt relieved. I went to the front door and started to ring the bell. Through the glass I could see into the living room, and my hand froze in mid-air. I saw my Dad sitting on the sofa, and he wasn't alone. There was a woman snuggled close to him. She was very pretty and when Dad kissed her, it tore my heart in two. He was only supposed to do that with my mother.

Something distracted them and they quickly separated. A little girl, perhaps six, ran into the room and jumped into the woman's lap. Dad tousled her hair and poked her in the ribs. They seemed like such a happy family. They seemed just the way we'd been once.

I took my hand away from the bell. I'd only wanted to show Dad that I loved him and wanted him back in my life. But he already seemed to have another life, a life that had nothing to do with me. And what did Mom do on those weekends when I was with Dad? Maybe she had a boyfriend. Maybe this was the future Mom had talked about. But where did that leave me? Where did I belong?

Maybe I didn't belong anywhere. If Mom and Dad had made new lives for themselves, then perhaps that's what I needed to do, too. I had to go out and meet new people, find a new relationship where I'd fit in. There didn't seem to be room for me in their lives anymore.

I got on my bike and rode slowly away, my mind filled with confusing thoughts. When I came to a gas station, I stopped and bought a soda. There was a big cargo van parked there, its back doors open. I didn't even think about what I was doing. I just threw my bag in and climbed in after it, hiding myself behind some boxes. Some time later the engine started and the truck lurched off. I didn't know it, but I was on my way to the city.

It was hot in the back of the truck and all the bouncing around gave me a headache. I kept thinking someone would discover me, but the truck went all the way into the city without stopping. Then it began making lots of stops for traffic lights. I waited for an opportunity when there wasn't much traffic behind us, then I jumped out. Nobody yelled at me, and I quickly crossed the street to the safety of the sidewalk.

As the truck drove away, I looked around to get my bearings. There were a lot of tall buildings there, and the traffic was heavy and noisy. It was all very confusing. For a moment I was frightened. I'd always had a family to depend on. Then I remembered that I didn't have a family anymore. I was going to have to make my own life now, just as my parents were doing.

I must've stood there for several minutes trying to decide what to do. Then I noticed a police car approaching, and it seemed to be slowing down. Maybe he thought I looked lost, or maybe he thought I resembled a missing persons photo he had seen. Time to move on. I started walking with a purposeful look on my face. There were a lot of people on the sidewalks, and it wasn't difficult to blend in with the crowd. The cop car kept going.

After a few blocks I came to a bus station that had a lunch counter, so I went in and bought a hamburger. It wasn't a very clean place. The counter was sticky and the floor was littered with old newspapers and Styrofoam cups. The waitress wore a stained and wrinkled uniform, and she had dirty fingernails. It wasn't the sort of place I was used to. The customers didn't seem like the sort of people who would complain about such things, though. They were even more shabbily dressed and dirty, and they smelled awful.

"Welcome to the big city," someone said. I turned to see a pretty girl of about twenty-five sitting on the stool next to me. She had nice hair and was wearing faded blue jeans. She was clean, though, and smelled of perfume instead of sweat.

"How did you know I just got here?"

"It shows," she said simply. "You can't fool people about something like that."

I thought of the cop I'd seen and nodded. I was going to have to be careful or I would end up back home very quickly.

"You waiting for somebody?" she asked. "Somebody supposed to meet you?"

"Yes," I lied. It didn't seem wise to reveal too much information to a stranger, even though she did seem rather nice. "They must've been delayed."

"Sure," the girl said. "Delayed forever. Nobody's going to meet you here because nobody knows where you are. You're a runaway, aren't you?"

I turned away and stared at my plate. It had egg stains on it. I thought about how mom would go ballistic if the dishes weren't properly cleaned.

"I was a runaway, too," the girl said. "I ran away three years ago, when I was fourteen."

That made me look at her again. If she were really only seventeen, she looked much older. Maybe she did that deliberately. There were a lot of advantages to looking a little older.

"What happened?" I asked.

"My mom's boyfriend was getting a little too friendly."

"Nobody tried to find you?"

"No." She laughed. "At least they didn't try very hard. My name's Stephanie." She held out her hand to me, the way one adult would greet another.

"Jenna," I said, shaking her hand.

"That's a nice name," she said. She took a drink of her soda, then made a face. "I bet they water down the water here."

"It's not like my mom's food," I said, looking distastefully at what was left of my sandwich.

"You better get used to that," Stephanie said. "It's hard living on the streets. You might need some help. Or at least some advice."

"What kind of advice?"

"Like staying away from drugs. I can tell by looking at you that you haven't gotten in to that. You might think that you never will, and that would be a mistake. It's easy to fall into the drug trap. It sneaks up on you."

"I think I can manage to do that," I said, a little disappointed. For years adults had been telling me to stay away from drugs. I thought that Stephanie, who had spent time on the streets, would have something more profound to say.

"They all say that." She took another sip of her drink, then pushed it away in disgust. "The other thing you want to do is stay away from pimps. They tell you that they'll give you protection, but all they do is take your money. They can't protect you from anything. The only person who can do that is you. You have to learn to have a sixth sense about trouble. That's how you stay alive on the streets."

I wrinkled my brow. What was all this talk about pimps? I'd heard about them on TV shows. They were like managers for women who sold their bodies. There was no reason for her to be telling me anything about that sort of stuff. I certainly wasn't going to use drugs or be a prostitute. I was just a runaway, one of thousands. I was a homeless person. That's all living on the street meant—that you didn't have a permanent home to go to.

"That really doesn't have anything to do with me," I said. "I can get enough handouts to buy food. All I need is a place to stay."

Stephanie turned toward me and stared long and hard. Her eyes were like X-ray beams shooting through me. It made me very uncomfortable, and I began to squirm.

"Honey, you're nothing but fresh meat," Stephanie said. "The best thing you could do is buy a bus ticket and go back home."

I shook my head. "I can't do that. I don't have a home anymore."

"You'd better come with me, then. Otherwise, you're going to suddenly realize you're not in Kansas anymore, and you're not even going to have Toto for company."

"Huh?" I had no idea what she was talking about. Nevertheless, I left the bus station with her. There seemed to be no reason not to. Stephanie knew her way around. Maybe she could help me find a place in this strange city.

Stephanie lived in an abandoned building with no electricity or water. "At least it's dry," she said. "And safe. If anyone tries to get in here, they'll make enough noise to give you plenty of warning. There's a couple ways out if that happens. I'll show you."

We spent the next several hours going through the building and the surrounding neighborhood. She wanted me to get familiar with my new surroundings. "This is where you live now. You'll have to know it like the back of your hand. Nobody's going to help you here, so you have to do for yourself."

Toward evening, we went back to the building and Stephanie got ready for work. She put on seamed fishnet stockings and a tight, short dress. She didn't have to tell me what kind of work she did.

"You'll be by yourself for a while," she said. "But you'll be safe as long as you stay put. I'll be back by two or three."

I remember being a little disappointed that my newfound friend was nothing more than a hooker. I couldn't imagine why she would want to sell her body to strangers. She seemed too kind and decent for that. It took a while for me to realize that this was about the only way for a runaway to earn money.

Stephanie and I soon became close friends, and I depended entirely on her for my support. She never said a word about that, but after a while it began to make me feel guilty.

"It's not fair," I said. "I should be doing something to help out around here."

"You keep the place clean. And you're always here for me to talk to. That helps more than you know."

"That's not what I mean. I should be bringing in some money."

She gave me a hard look, then nodded her head slightly. "Come on. I want to show you something."

She took me over to Eleventh and Main, where she usually worked. Even though it was a bit early, there were girls hanging out, looking for customers. You could tell by the way they were dressed what they were doing. Plenty of cars were pulling up to the curb and the men were calling to the girls. Some of them even tried to get my attention. Even though I ignored them, it made me feel uncomfortable.

"So this is your little friend I've heard about," one of the girls said.

"This is my cousin, Jenna. She's staying with me for a while."

"The johns will really like her. She could make a real killing out here."

Stephanie shook her head. "She's too young for that. I'm just showing her around town. Come on," she said to me.

"Why did you take me there?" I asked a few minutes later.

"Because I wanted you to know what it's going to be like. You keep thinking you can beg for money, or find aluminum cans or something. That's not going to bring in any money. Out here, you have to work with what you've got, and we both know what we've got. That's what you're going to have to use. Get ready for it, or get ready to go back home. That's your choice, Jenna."

It was difficult to avoid the other girls, even during the day. They began taunting me, calling me a moocher and a loafer. They were a bit jealous of me, I think, because Stephanie had always been a loner.

"Leave her alone," Stephanie said. "Jenna has to make up her own mind. Don't try to force her into anything."

"Huh," one of the girls said. "I was forced into it. How's she any different?"

"You had the same choice Jenna has—the street or back home."

"That's not much of a choice," the girl responded.

"It's still a choice," Stephanie said. "Give her time to think it over."

The girls left me alone after that. I'd been doing plenty of thinking, too. It seemed to me that if my parents had been really trying to find me, they probably would've done so. That meant there wasn't much point in my going back. And even if they had been looking, that wouldn't make things any different. I'd still be in the way. Stephanie had become the best friend I'd ever had, and I didn't want to leave her. And, in a way, I think she needed me as much as I needed her. I'd already found what I was looking for—a place to belong.

"Maybe you need to give your parents a second chance," Stephanie said. "Things are always difficult after a divorce. In a few years, you might see things differently. If things don't work out, you can always come back here."

"Do you really think I should go back, Stephanie?"

"I do. You don't belong here. Look at the people you see. All the girls are on drugs. Some of them have babies. This is no kind of life for a girl like you."

"What about you? You're not like the others."

"I've got no place to go back to," she said. "I have to stick it out until I get a chance at something better. Find a decent job someplace. I'd like to go back to school again, make something of myself. I've saved up quite a bit of money." A faraway look came into her eyes. "You have to have patience. And that's why you need to go back and try again."

And that's what I would've done if things hadn't happened to complicate my plans.

Stephanie usually came home around three in the morning, sometimes a bit later. When five o'clock came and went, I began to get worried. I felt so helpless simply waiting there for her, so I ventured out. Maybe some of the girls would still be hanging around and could tell me what had happened.

The corner where they worked was deserted. At this early hour the city was beginning to stir, which meant that business hours for the streetwalkers was over. The police didn't like the girls flaunting their wares in the daylight hours.

I walked the familiar streets, hoping to find some sign of her. She may have gotten sick and was unable to return home. I decided to call the hospitals to see if she'd been taken there. The other possibility was that she'd been arrested. I knew where Stephanie kept her money, and there might be enough to bail her out. If I showed up at the police station, they'd probably keep me, but that was all right. I'd do that for my friend. I was ready to go home anyway.

I found a pay phone and searched my pockets for some coins. I'd try the hospitals first. Then I noticed Doreen, one of the girls, motioning to me from a doorway.

"Where's Stephanie?" I asked. "She hasn't come home."

"I know," she said. "She never came back from her last trick."

"What do you mean? Why wouldn't she come back?"

"Because she can't," Doreen said. "These things happen once in a while. You can never be sure who you're getting in the car with."

I shook my head. Doreen was one of the addicts, and she may have been on drugs. She wasn't making any sense to me. "I don't understand what you're saying. What things happen?" I asked.

Doreen grabbed my arm and pulled me farther into the doorway. She'd seen a police car cruising the streets.

"I mean," she said, squeezing my arm so tightly it hurt, "that sometimes the guys want more than sex. Sometimes they like to hurt people. Or worse. You're not ever going to see Stephanie again. Not alive, anyway."

Her words sent a chill down my spine. There were always stories about the girls disappearing, and it was difficult to know exactly what that meant. A lot of the girls were runaways and simply moved on. Quite a few of them died from drug overdoses. And sometimes the girls would be murdered. The bodies would be found months later, long after they were recognizable. Cops didn't waste much time trying to find out who killed a hooker. They had too many other things to do.

"Stephanie can't be dead," I said. That was the sort of thing that happened to other people. Stephanie wasn't like these girls. I tore myself loose and backed away from her. "Maybe she's been arrested."

"Stephanie's dead," Doreen said. "The word's all over the street. You're lucky you got out of your place when you did. One of the pimps thought Stephanie had money hidden there and he went to look for it. If you'd been there you probably would've gotten hurt."

There was a painful lump in my throat and tears were running down my face. "It's not true. Stephanie can't be dead. She's not one of you."

I ran away from Doreen and her awful lies.

Stephanie will be waiting for me, I told myself. If not, I'll wait for her, because I know she'll come back.

Stephanie wasn't there, but someone clearly had been. The place had been turned upside down. All of our clothes had been tossed on the floor and cut to shreds. The broken floorboards told me Stephanie's money was gone. In the corner were some belongings that weren't ours. Someone had decided to take over our apartment. It wasn't safe for me to stay there any longer.

Within the space of a few hours I'd been thrown into the same predicament as when I arrived—no money, food, or shelter. The only way to get back home would be to call and have someone fetch me. And that's probably what I should've done. Only I felt that I would be abandoning Stephanie that way. I couldn't believe that she was dead. There had to be some other explanation. If she needed my help, I intended to be there for her, the way she'd been for me. I had to hang around long enough to convince myself she was really gone. I owed her that much.

"How you gonna make it on the streets?" Doreen asked when I told her what had happened. "Ain't nobody to baby-sit you now. You'll have to earn your way, just like the rest of us."

"I know," I said quietly. I'd been giving that some serious thought. I knew I wouldn't have any trouble attracting the men, even though I didn't have much of a figure. A lot of them liked younger girls, and would pay extra for them. Did I really want to take that next step and sell myself to strangers?

Back home, my friends and I had giggled over the stories we'd heard about some of the older girls. A lot of them, we knew, had done it, and some of them had done it with a lot of different boys. Whenever you went steady with a boy, it almost always meant sleeping with him. Having sex was often a casual thing, and was really just a matter of getting started. A lot of the girls who'd started were only a few years older than me.

It's no big deal, I told myself. The first time, maybe. Sex and love are two separate things that sometimes can be combined. Most of the girls working the streets have boyfriends.

If that's what it took to stay there, then I could do it. I was too young to find any kind of job, and I was going to need money very soon.

"My pimp will take you in," Doreen said. "He'll see that you get a place to stay. He'll protect you. That's what happened to Stephanie. She didn't have nobody to protect her."

I shook my head. Stephanie had warned me about that. The pimps tried to get their girls hooked on drugs. That's how they kept them in line.

"I'll do it on my own," I said. "Once you're in that car, there's no one to protect you but yourself." You had to learn who to go with and who not to go with. I'd seen how the girls worked, and had often correctly second guessed them. I had a pretty good idea about what I was getting into. I wasn't the innocent girl I'd been a few months ago.

Finding a place to stay wasn't as difficult as you might think. Stephanie and I had lived for months in an abandoned building, and there were lots of old, empty buildings in the neighborhood. It was only a matter of finding one that wasn't being used by anyone else, one that wasn't so convenient that you'd have trouble with the drug pushers.

I found a place about six blocks from the corner where the girls worked. It was an old printing factory whose roof had caved in, so that didn't provide much protection from the elements. After a bit of exploring I discovered a basement, and although it was damp and didn't get much light, it had two exits. With a bit of work, this would be my new home.

All I had were the clothes on my back—a pair of blue jeans and a buttoned blouse. This wasn't the sort of clothing that would attract the kind of attention I was looking for. I cut off the jeans, making them very short, then unbuttoned my top and tied the ends together. The result showed off my sleek, slender legs and my flat stomach. It projected exactly the sort of image I needed to make my way on Main Street. With a few snips of the scissors, I had become a working girl.

That first night wasn't very pleasant. I lost my virginity to a man old enough to be my grandfather. He used me over and over, drooling on me like a piece of meat, which I was. What I was doing sickened me, but the night was still young. There were two other men I went with, and when I went home I had two hundred dollars in my pocket. I took the next three days off. I was so sore I could barely walk.

I used my earnings to buy food, clothing, and a sleeping bag. And instead of hiding my extra money, I opened a savings account. It wasn't that difficult to do, and it would be a lot safer than keeping it on the premises.

And that's how I became a streetwalker, a lady of the night, a hooker—whatever you want to call me. Some of the other girls began to resent me because I became so popular with the men. My figure never filled out much. If I'd been in school, that would've been a problem. Here, it was an advantage. The johns thought I was a pre-teen, and that meant I could charge extra money. If grown men wanted me to be an enthusiastic twelve-year-old virgin, I could do that, night after night. The customer was always right.

I learned the ways of the street like the back of my hand. I knew which cops I had to avoid, and which ones I had to entertain. I've gotten in cars with young men and old ones, prominent citizens and city officials, drunken soldiers and bums. It was all in a night's work.

And all the time I kept my eyes open for Stephanie, for any sign of her. Somewhere there had to be a trace of her, some lead I could follow. If she were able to come back I knew she would, and yet it was difficult for me to accept that she was dead—despite the fact that several other girls had been found in shallow graves.

"They're never satisfied," Doreen said to me when one of our group had been found in a ditch. "They always have to have that little extra thing. They don't care if it's your last breath. We're not really people to them."

As the months went by, I slowly got used to the idea of Stephanie not coming back. One day I'd learn of her decomposed body being discovered somewhere, and the police would say that they had no suspects and no leads. If that ever happened, then I'd be there to claim her body. For whatever it was worth, I would be there to say that I had once known that person, that she'd been my friend, and that she mattered. Every human being, no matter how low he or she sinks, still has some worth. Otherwise, our society doesn't mean a thing.

I seldom thought of my parents. Of course, I remembered all the good times there had been when we were all together. But those times were over. Mom and Dad had created separate lives for themselves, and so had I. There really wasn't anything for me to go back to anymore. We were three perfect strangers. The only strangers who interested me now were the ones who paid cash.

And that's the story of my life so far. I'm only fourteen, so it's not much of a story.

A man in a van pulls to the curb and is motioning to me. He might be a regular john who will pay me for services rendered, or he might be someone out to do me harm—maybe even kill me. All I have to go on is my experience, and I know that experience only means that so far nothing has happened to me.

That's how my working day goes. There is always the decision: Is this the guy I get in the car with, or not? They all flash money, and I always need money. How can you tell who is out to hurt you? I always look at their eyes. That seems to be the doorway to the soul. The other girls scoff at this idea. It's the hands, they say, or the smile, or how clean they keep their cars. You hear all kinds of advice. In the end, all you have is a gut feeling.

I think that when Stephanie got in that car for the last time, she had a gut feeling everything would be okay. She'd been wrong. Mistakes happen.

The man before me has a nice smile and gentle eyes. His car is clean. He is holding money in his well-manicured hands.

I get in the car. This man will give me another day's wages. Or, if I have chosen wrong, then maybe he can tell me what happened to my best friend, Stephanie.

How strange, I sometimes think, that I could find the answer to one mystery, only to become one myself. I don't think anyone will look for me. I haven't made any close friends here on Main Street. People here are looking for survival, not friendship. And I'm still looking for a place to belong.

THE END